Ballantine Books' publication of Three Corvettes a few months ago met with the eager response of readers who first came to know this author's work on publication of his international best seller, THE CRUEL SEA.

NOW

Ballantine Books is proud to bring to this new generation of readers the second work in Nicholas Monsarrat's trilogy of stories about his wartime experience as an officer in corvettes in the North Atlantic in World War II.

THIS IS THE TRUE STORY

of the war that Monsarrat fought—
of the dangers of hunting subs and protecting convoys during the darkest days of the war—
of the courage and pride of the men who served in the Navy's smallest ships—
told with the boldness and vividness for which this author has achieved his fame.

H.M.S. MARLBOROUGH WILL ENTER HARBOR

by

Nicholas Monsarrat

Ballantine Books   **New York**

Ballantine Books, Inc.
101 Fifth Avenue, New York 3, N. Y.

H.M.S. MARLBOROUGH WILL ENTER HARBOR

Chapter One

~~~~~~~~~~~~~~~~~~~~~~~~~~~~~~~~~

THE SLOOP *Marlborough,* 1,200
tons, complement 8 officers and 130 men, was
torpedoed at dusk on the last day of 1942 while
on independent passage from Iceland to the
Clyde. She was on her way home for refit, and
for the leave that went with it, after a four-
teen-month stretch of North Atlantic convoy
escort with no break, except for routine boiler-
cleaning. Three weeks' leave to each watch—
that had been the buzz going round the ship's
company when they left Reykjavik after taking in the last convoy; but many of them never
found out how much truth there was in that
buzz, for the torpedo struck at the worst moment, with two-thirds of the ship's company

having tea below decks, and when it exploded under the forward mess-deck at least sixty of them were killed outright.

H.M.S. *Marlborough* was an old ship, seventeen years old, and she took the outrage as an old lady of breeding should. At the noise and jar of the explosion a delicate shudder went all through her: then as her speed fell off there was stillness, while she seemed to be making an effort to ignore the whole thing: and then, brought face to face with the fury of this mortal attack, gradually and disdainfully she conceded the victory.

The deck plating of the fo'c'sle buckled and sagged, pulled downwards by the weight of the anchors and cables: all this deck, indeed, crumpled as far as the four-inch gun-mounting, which toppled forwards until the gun-muzzles were pointing foolishly at the sea; a big lurch tore loose many of the ammunition lockers and sent them cascading over the side. Until the way of her sixteen knots fell off, there were cruching noises as successive bulkheads took the weight of water, butted at it for a moment, and then gave in; and thus, after a space, she lay—motionless, cruelly hit, two hundred miles southwest of the Faroes and five hundred miles from home.

So far it had been an affair of metal: now swiftly it became an affair of men. From forward came muffled shouting—screaming, some of it—borne on the wind down the whole length of the ship, to advertise the shambles buried below. The dazed gun's crew from "A" gun, which had been directly over the explosion, climbed down from their sagging platform and drew off aft. There was a noise of trampling running feet from all over the ship: along alley ways, up ladders leading from the untouched spaces aft: confused voices, tossed to and fro by the wind, called as men tried to find out how bad the damage was, what the orders were, whether their friends had been caught or not.

On the upper deck, near the boats and at the foot of the bridge-ladders, the clatter and slur of feet and voices reached its climax. In the few moments before a firm hand was taken, with every light in the ship out and only the shock of the explosion as a guide to what had happened, there was confusion, noisy and urgent: the paramount need to move quickly clashed with indecision and doubt as to where that move could best be made. The dusk, the rising sea, the bitterly cold wind, which carried an acrid smell in sharp eddying puffs, were all part of this discordant aftermath: the iron trampling of those racing feet all over the ship bound it together, co-ordinating fear into a vast uneasy whole, a spur for panic if panic ever showed itself.

It never did show itself. The first disciplined reaction, one of many such small reassurances to reach the bridge, was the quartermaster's voice, admirably matter-of-fact, coming up the wheel-house voice-pipe: "Gyro compass gone dead, sir!" The midshipman, who shared the watch with the First Lieutenant and was at that moment licking a lip split open on the edge of the glass dodger, looked round uncertainly, found he was the only officer on the bridge, and answered: "Very good. Steer by magnetic," before he realized the futility of this automatic order. Then he jerked his head sideways, level with another voice-pipe, the one leading to the Captain's cabin, and called: "Captain, sir!"

There was no answer. Probably the Captain was on his way up already. Christ, suppose he's been killed, though. . . . The midshipman called again: "Captain, sir!" and a voice behind him said: "All right, Mid. I heard it."

He turned round, to find the comforting bulk of the Captain's duffle coat outlined against the dusk. It was not light enough to see the expression on his face, nor was there anything in his voice to give a clue to it. It did not occur to the midshipman to speculate about this, in any case: for him, this was simply the Captain, the man he had been waiting for, the man on whom every burden could now be squarely placed.

"Torpedo, sir."

"Yes."

The Captain moving with purpose but without hurry, stepped up onto the central compass platform, glanced once round him— and sat down. There was something special in that act of sitting down, there in the middle of the noise and movement reaching the bridge from all over the ship, and everyone near him caught it. The Captain, on the bridge, sitting in the Captain's chair. Of course: that was what they had been waiting for. . . . It was the beginning, the tiny tough centre, of control and order. Soon it would spread outwards.

"Which side was it from?"

"Port, sir. Just under 'A' gun."

"Tell the engine-room what's happened. . . . Where is the First Lieutenant?"

"He must have gone down, sir. I suppose he's with the Damage Control Party."

Up the voice-pipe came the quartermaster's voice again: "She won't come round, sir. The wheel's hard a-starboard."

"Never mind." The Captain turned his head slightly. "Pilot!"

A figure, bent over the chart table behind him, straightened up. "Sir?"

"Work out our position, and we'll send a signal."

"Just getting it out now."

The Captain bent forward to the voice-pipe again. "Bosun's Mate!"

"Sir?"

"Find the First Lieutenant. He'll be forrard somewhere. Tell him to report the damage as soon as he can."

"Aye, aye, sir."

That, at least, was a small space cleared. . . . Under him the ship felt sluggish and helpless; on the upper deck the voices clamoured, from below the cries still welled up. He looked round him, trying in the increasing darkness

12

to find out who was on the bridge. Not everyone he expected to see, not all the men who should have collected at such a moment, were there. The signalman and the bridge messenger. Two lookouts. Bridger, his servant, standing just behind him. Pilot and the Mid. Someone else he could not make out.

He called: "Coxswain?"

There was a pause, and then a voice said: "He was below, sir."

"Who's that?"

"Adams, sir."

Adams was the Chief Bosun's Mate, and the second senior rating on board. After a moment the Captain said:

"If he doesn't get out, you take over, Adams. . . . You'd better organize three or four of your quartermasters, for piping round the ship. I'll want you to stay by me. If there's anything to be piped you can pass it on."

"Aye, aye, sir."

There was too much noise on the upper deck, for a start. But perhaps it would be better if he spoke to them over the loud-hailer. Once more the Captain turned his head.

"Yeoman!"

Another pause, and then the same definitive phrase, this time from the signalman of the watch: "He was below, sir."

A wicked lurch, and another tearing noise from below, covered the silence after the words were spoken. But the Captain seemed to take them in his stride.

"See if the hailer's working," he said to the signalman.

"I've got the position, sir," said Haines, the navigating officer. "Will you draft a signal?"

"Get on to the W/T office and see if they can send it, first."

"The hailer's all right, sir," said the signalman. "Batteries still working."

"Very good. Train the speaker aft."

He clicked on the microphone, and from force of habit blew through it sharply. A healthy roar told him that the thing was in order. He cleared his throat.

"Attention, please! This is the Captain speaking." His voice, magnified without distortion, overcame the wind and the shouting, which died away to nothing, "I want to tell you what's happened. We've been torpedoed on the port side, under 'A' gun. The First Lieutenant is finding out about the damage now. I want you all to keep quiet, and move about as little as possible, until I know what the position is. . . . 'X' gun's crew will stand fast, the rest of the watch-on-deck clear away the boats and rafts ready for lowering. Do *not* start lowering, or do anything else, until I give the order over this hailer, or until you hear the pipe. That is all."

The speaker clicked off, leaving silence on the bridge and all over the upper deck. Only the voices hidden below still called. He became aware that Haines was standing by his elbow, preparing to speak.

"What is it, Pilot?"

"It's the W/T office, sir. They can't transmit."

"Who's down there?"

"The leading tel., sir. The P.O. tel. was below." (That damned phrase again. If those two messes, the Chief's and the Petty Officer's, were both written off, it was going to play hell with organizing the next move, whatever it was.) "But he knows what he's doing, sir," Haines went on. "The dynamo's been thrown off the board, but the set's had a hell of a knock anyway."

"Go down yourself and make sure." Haines,

as well as being navigating officer, was an electrical expert, and this was in fact his department.

"Aye, aye, sir."

"Midshipman!"

"Sir?"

"Pass the word to the Gunnery Officer—"

"I'm here, sir." Guns' tall figure loomed up behind him. "I've been looking at 'A' gun."

"Well?"

"It's finished, I'm afraid, sir."

Guns knew his job, and the Captain did not ask him to elaborate. Instead he said:

"I think we'll try a little offensive action while we're waiting, in case those—come up to take a look at us." He considered. "Close up on 'X' gun, go into local control, fire a spread of star-shell through this arc"—he indicated the port bow and beam—"and let fly if you see anything. I'll leave the details to you."

"Aye, aye, sir."

Guns clumped off down the ladder on his way aft. It was one of his idiosyncracies to wear street-cleaner's thigh boots with thick wooden soles, and his movements up and down the ship were easily traceable, earning indeed a good deal of fluent abuse from people who were trying to get to sleep below. As the heavy footfalls receded aft, the Captain stood up and leant over the port side of the bridge, staring down at the tumbling water. There was nothing to be seen of the main area of the damage, which was hidden by the outward flare of the bows; but the ship had less freedom of movement now—she was deeper, more solidly settled in the water. They must have taken tons of it in the ripped-up spaces forward: the fo'c'sle covering them looked like a slowly crumbling ruin. It was about time the First Lieutenant came through with his report. If they had to—

"What's that?" he asked suddenly.

A thin voice was calling "Bridge, Bridge," from one of the voice-pipes. He bent down to the row nearest to him, but from none of them did the voice issue clearly. Behind him the midshipman was conducting the same search on his side. The voice went on calling "Bridge, Bridge, Bridge," in a patient monotone. It was the Captain's servant, Bridger, who finally traced it—a voice-pipe low down on the deck, its anti-spray cover still clipped on.

The man bent down to it and snapped back the cover. "Bridge here."

A single murmured sentence answered him. Bridger looked up to the Captain. "It's the Engineer Officer, sir, speaking from the galley flat."

The Captain bent down. A waft of bitter fume-laden air met his nostrils. "Yes, Chief?"

"I'm afraid Number One got caught by that last bulkhead, sir."

"What happened? I heard it go a little while back."

"We thought it would hold, sir." The level voice, coming from the heart of the ruined fo'c'sle, had an apologetic note, as if the speaker, even in that shambles, had had the cool honesty to convict himself of an error of judgment. "It did look like holding for a bit, too. Number One was with the damage control party, between the seamen's mess-deck and the bathrooms. They'd shut the watertight door behind them, and were just going to shore up, when the forrard bulkhead went." Chief paused. "You know what it's like, sir. We can't get at them without opening up."

"Can't do that now, Chief."

"No, sir."

"Can you hear anything?"

"Not now."

"How many were there with the First Lieutenant?"

"Fourteen, sir. Mostly stokers." There was another pause. "I took charge down here, sir. We're shoring up the next one."

"What do you think of it?"

"Not too good. It's badly strained already, and leaking down one seam." There was, now, a slightly sharpened note in the voice travelling up from below. "There's a hell of a mess down here, sir. And if this one goes, that'll mean the whole lot."

"Yes, I know." The Captain thought quickly, while overhead and to port the sea was suddenly lit up by a cold yellow glare— the first spread of star-shell, four slowly dropping lights shadowing their spinning parachutes against the cloud overhead. Very pretty. . . . The news from below could hardly have been worse: it added up to fully a third of the ship flooded, all the forward mess-decks cut off, fourteen men drowned at one stroke, and God knows how many more caught by the original explosion. "Look here, Chief, I don't want any more men lost like that. You must use your own judgment about getting out in a hurry. See how the shoring up goes, and let me know as soon as you can if you think it'll hold."

"All right, sir."

"We're firing star-shell at the moment, to see if there's anything on the surface. 'X' gun may be firing independently, any time from now on."

"All right, sir."

"Take care of yourself, Chief."

He could almost hear the other man smiling at what was, from the Captain, an unexpected remark. "I'll do that, sir."

The voice-pipe went dead. Walking back to his chair, the Captain allowed himself a moment of profound depression and regret. The First Lieutenant gone. A good kid, doing his first big job in the Navy and tremendously keen to do it properly. With a young wife, too —the three of them had had dinner at the Adelphi in Liverpool, not two weeks ago. There was a bad letter to be written there, later on. And the loss might make a deal of difference to the next few hours.

The star-shell soared and dropped again. Sitting in his chair, waiting for Chief's report, listening to the green seas slapping and thumping against the side as *Marlborough* sagged downwind in the wave troughs with a new, ugly motion, he was under no illusions as to what the next few hours might bring, and the chances of that "bad letter" ever being written by himself. But that was not what he was now concentrating on: that was not in the mapped-out programme. . . . This was the moment for which the Navy had long been preparing him: for years his training and experience had had this precise occasion in view; that was why he was a commander, and the Captain of *Marlborough* when she was hit. Taking charge, gauging chances, foreseeing the next eventuality and if necessary forestalling it—none of it could take him by surprise, any more than could the chapter headings of a favourite book. When the moment had arrived he had recognized it instantly, and the sequence of his behaviour had lain before him like a familiar pattern, of which he now had to take the tenth or twentieth tracing. He had not been torpedoed before, but no matter: tucked away in his mind and brain there had always been a picture of a torpedoed ship, and of himself as, necessarily, the key figure in this picture. Now that the curtain was drawn, and the image became the reality, he simply had to play his assigned part with as much intelligence, skill, and endurance as he could muster. The loss of the First Lieutenant and over half the ship's company already was a bitter stroke, both personally and professionally: it would return in full force later; but for the moment it was only a debit item which had to be fitted into the evolving picture.

"Signalman!"

"Sir."

"Get the Gunnery Officer on the quarter-deck telephone."

A pause. More star-shell, reflected on a waste of cold tumbling water, dropped slowly till they were drowned in darkness again. There wasn't really much point in going on with the illumination now: the U-boat probably thought they had other ships in company ready to counter-attack, and had sheered off. She had, indeed, cause to be satisfied, without pursuing the advantage further. . . .

"Gunnery Officer on the telephone, sir."

The Captain took the proffered receiver. "Guns?"

"Yes, sir?"

"I'm afraid Number One has been killed. I want you to take over."

"Oh—all right, sir."

Hearing the shocked surprise in his voice, the Captain remembered that the two of them had been very good friends. But that, again, was something to be considered later: only the bald announcement was part of the present pattern. He continued:

"I think you had better stay aft, as if we were still at full action stations. Chief is in charge of damage control forrard. Stop star-shell now—I take it you've seen nothing."

"Nothing, sir."

"Right. You'd better have all the depth-charges set to safe—in fact have the primers withdrawn and dropped over the side. And I want someone to have a look at our draught-marks aft."

"I've just had them checked, sir. There's nothing to go on, I'm afraid: they're right clear of the water."

"Are the screws out of the water too?"

"Can't see in this light, sir. The top blades, probably."

"Right. Get going on those depth-charges."

The Captain handed back the receiver, at the same time saying to the signalman: "Get your confidential books in the weighted bags, ready for ditching. And tell the W/T office to do the same."

"Aye, aye, sir."

"Bridger."

"Yes, sir."

"Go down and get the black hold-all, and come back here."

"Aye, aye, sir." Bridger's tough, unemotional expression did not alter, but his shoulders stiffened instinctively. He knew what the order meant. The black hold-all was, in his own phrase, the scram-bag: it held a bottle of brandy, morphine ampoules, a first-aid kit, some warm clothes, and a few personal papers. It had been tucked away in a corner of the skipper's cabin for nearly three years. It was as good as a ticket over the side. They'd start swimming any moment now.

The report from aft about the draught-marks had certainly quickened the tempo a little: his orders to Bridger and to the signal-man were an endorsement of this. But quick tempo or slow, there was still the same number of things to be fitted into the available time, the same number of lines in the pattern to be traced. Now, in the darkness, as he turned to the next task, very little noise or movement reached the bridge from anywhere in the ship: only a sound of hammering from deep below (the damage-control party busy on their shoring job), a voice calling "Take a turn, there," as the whaler was swung out, the endless thump and surge of the waves driving down wind—only these were counter distraction in the core of heart and brain which the bridge had now become. Indeed, the Captain was much less conscious of these than of the heavy breathing of Adams, the Chief Bosun's Mate, who stood by his elbow as close and attentive as a spaniel at the butts. Adams had heard the order to Bridger, and had guessed what it meant: it had aroused, not his curiosity—matters were past such a faint reaction as curiosity now—but the same tough determination as the Captain himself had felt. They were both men of the same stamp: seamen first, human beings afterwards; the kind of men whom *Marlborough*, in her extremity, most needed and most deserved.

"Mid!"

"Yes, sir?"

"Go along to the sick-bay, and—"

One of the voice-bells rang sharply. The

midshipman listened for a moment, and then said: "That's the doctor now, sir."

The Captain bent down. "Yes, doc?"

"I wanted to report about casualties, sir."

"What's the position?"

"I've got nine down here, sir. Burns, mostly. One stoker with a broken arm. I got a stretcher-party organized, and brought them down aft."

"I was hoping there'd be more."

"Afraid not, sir."

"Do you need any hands to help you?"

"No, I'm all right, sir. I've got one sick-berth attendant—Jamieson was caught forrard, I'm afraid—and the leading steward is giving a hand."

"Very well. But you'll have to start moving them, I'm afraid. Get them on the upper deck, on the lee side. Ask Guns to lend you some hands from 'X' gun."

There was a pause. Then the doctor's voice came through again, more hesitantly. "They shouldn't really be moved, sir, unless—"

"That's what I meant. You understand?"

"Yes, sir."

"Send the walking cases up to the boat-deck, and see to the others yourself. Divide them up between the two boats. I'll leave the details to you."

"Very well, sir."

Thank God for a good doctor, anyway—as bored, cynical, and impatient as most naval doctors were for three-quarters of their time, with nothing to do but treat warts and censor the mail: and then, on an occasion like this, summoning all the resource and skill that had been kept idle, and throwing them instantly into the breech. The doctor was going to be an asset during the next few hours. So, indeed, was every officer and man left to the ship.

He would have liked to muster the remaining hands, to see how many the explosion had caught and how many he had left to work with; but that would disrupt things too much, at a time when there must be no halting in the desperate race to save the ship or, at least, as many of the remaining lives as possible. But as he sat back in his chair, waiting for what he was now almost sure must happen, the Captain reviewed his officers one by one, swiftly tabulating their work at this moment, speculating whether they could be better employed. Number One was gone, of course. Guns in charge aft. Haines in the wireless office (time he was back, incidentally). Chief working the damage-control party—that was technically his responsibility anyway, and there was a first-class Chief E.R.A. in charge of the engine-room. The Mid. here on the bridge. The doctor with his hands full in the sick-bay. Merrett—the Captain frowned suddenly. Where the devil was Merrett? He'd forgotten all about him—and indeed it was easy to overlook the shy, newly joined sub who had startled the wardroom on his first night by remarking: "My father went to prison as a conscientious objector during the last war, so he's rather ashamed of me in this one," but had then relapsed into the negative, colourless attitude which seemed natural to him. Where had he got to now?

The Captain repeated the query aloud to the midshipman.

"I haven't seen him at all, sir," the latter answered. "He was in the wardroom when I came on watch. Shall I call them up?"

"Yes, do."

After a moment at one of the voice-pipes the midshipman came through with the answer: "He was there a moment ago, sir. They think he's on the upper deck somewhere."

"Send one of the bosun's mates to—" The

Captain paused. No, that might not be a good move. "See if you can find him, Mid., and ask him to come up here."

When the midshipman had left the bridge the Captain frowned again. Why in God's name had Merrett been in the wardroom a moment ago? What was he doing there at a time like this? Any sort of alarm or crisis meant that officers went to their action stations automatically: Merrett should have gone first to "A" gun, where he was in charge, and then, as that was out of action, up to the bridge for orders. Now all that was known of him was that he had been in the wardroom, right aft. The Captain hoped there was a good explanation, not the attack of nerves or the breakdown of self-control he had been guessing at when he sent the midshipman to find Merrett. He could understand such a thing happening— the boy was barely twenty, and this was his first trip—but they just could not afford it now.

His guess had been right: so much became obvious as soon as Merrett was standing in front of him. Even in the darkness, with the exact expression on his face blurred and shadowed, he seemed to manifest an almost exalted state of terror. The movements of foot and

29

hand, the twitching shoulders, the slight, un-controlled chattering of the teeth, the shine of sweat on the forehead—all were here, a distilla-tion of fear which would, in full daylight, have been horrible to look at. So that was it. . . . For a moment the Captain hesitated, trying to balance their present crucial danger, and his own controlled reaction to it, against the al-most unknown feelings of a boy, a landsman-turned-sailor, confronted with the same ordeal; but then the overriding necessity of everyone on board doing his utmost, swept away any readiness to make allowances for failure in this respect. The details, the pros and cons, the fine-drawn questions could wait; nothing but one hundred per cent effective-ness would suffice now, and that was what he must re-establish.

"Where have you been?" he asked curtly.

Merrett swallowed, looked across the shat-tered fo'c'sle to the wild sea, and drew no com-fort or reassurance from it. He said, in a dry strained voice: "I'm sorry, sir. I didn't know what to do, exactly."

"Then you should come and ask me. Do you expect me to come and tell you?" It was rough: it was, in Merrett's present state, brutally so:

but it was clearly dictated by the situation they were in. "Where were you when we were hit?"

"I'd just gone up to 'A' gun, sir."

"Must have shaken you up a bit." So much allowance, and no more, did the Captain make for what he could only guess at now—youth, uncertainty, self-distrust, perhaps an inherited horror of violence. "But I don't want to have to send for individual officers at a time like this. You understand?"

"Yes, sir." It was a whisper, almost a sigh. He'd been drinking whisky, too, the Captain thought. Well, that didn't matter as long as it had the right results; and this, and the tonic effect of giving him a definite job to do, could be put to the test now.

"Very well. . . . There's something I want you to do," he went on, changing his tone in such a way as to indicate clearly that a fresh start could now be made. "Go down to the boat-deck and see how they're getting on with the boats. They're to be swung out ready for lowering, and all the rafts cleared away as well. You'd better check up on the boats' crews, too: remember we've only got this one watch of seamen to play with, so far as we know. You'll want a coxswain, a stoker, and a bowman told off for the motor-boat, and a coxswain and a bowman for the whaler. Got that?"

"Yes, sir."

It seemed that he had: already he was making some attempt to take a grip on his body, and his voice was more under control. Watching him turn and make for the bridge-ladder, the Captain felt ready to bet that he would make a good job of it. The few minutes had not been wasted.

But they had been no more than an odd, irrelevant delay in the main flow of the current; and now, in quick succession, as if to re-establish the ordained pace of disaster, three more stages came and were passed. Bridger appeared with the black hold-all, and with something else which he handed to the Captain almost furtively. "Better have this, sir," he said, as the Captain's hand closed over it. It was his safety-light, which he had forgotten to clip onto his life-jacket—one of the small water-tight bulb-and-battery sets which were meant to be plugged in and switched on when in the water. The Captain took it with a grunt and fastened it on, his eyes turned instinctively to the black expanse of water washing and swirling round them. Yes, better have the light ready. . . .

Then Haines came up the ladder from below, starting to speak almost before he was on the bridge:

"I'm afraid they were right about the W/T set, sir," he began. "It's finished. And the main switchboard has blown, too. Even if we got the dynamo back on the board—"

"All right, Pilot," said the Captain suddenly. And then, to the figure he had discerned at the top of the ladder, the third messenger of evil, he said: "Yes, Chief?"

The engineer officer did not speak until he was standing close by the Captain, but there was no hesitation about his opening words. "I don't think it's any good, sir." He spoke with a clipped intensity, which did not disguise an exhaustion of spirit. "That bulkhead—it might go any minute, and she'll probably break in two when it happens. That means a lot more men caught, sir."

"You've shored up completely?"

"Yes, sir. But the space is too big, and the bulkhead was warped too much before we got the shores to it. It's working badly already. I can't see it holding more than another hour, if that."

"It's the last one worth shoring," said the Captain, almost to himself.

"Yes, sir." Chief hesitated. "I've still seven or eight hands down in the engine-room, I'd like to get them out in good time. Is that all right, sir?"

Chief was looking at him. They were all looking at him—Haines, the midshipman, the signalman, Adams, the look-outs, the hard-breathing Bridger—all waiting for the one plain order, which they now knew must come. Until that moment he had been refusing to look squarely at this order as it drew nearer and nearer; he could not believe that his loved ship must be given up, and even now, as he hesitated, and the men round him wondered, the idea still had no sort of reality about it. For this man on whom they all relied, this man to whom they attributed no feelings or qualities apart from the skill and forethought of seamanship, was not quite the stock figure, the thirty-eight-year-old R.N. commander, that they took him to be.

True, he fitted the normal mould well enough. He had always done so, from Dartmouth onwards, and the progress from mid-shipman to commander had followed its appointed course—twenty years of naval routine in which a mistake, a stepping-out-of-line, would have denied him his present rank. He never had stepped out of line; had been, and still was, normal about everything except this ship; but for her he had a special feeling, a romantic conception, which would have astounded the men waiting round him. It was not the Navy, or his high sense of duty, or the fact that he commanded her, which had given him this feeling: it was love.

The old *Marlborough*. . . . The Captain was not married, and if he had been it might not have made any difference: he was profoundly and exclusively in love with this ship, and the passion, fed especially on the dangers and ordeals of the past three war-years, left no room for a rival. It had started in 1926, when she was brand new and he had commissioned her: it had been his first job as First Lieutenant, and his proudest so far. She had been the very latest in ships then—a new sloop, Clyde-built, twin turbines, two four-inch guns (the twin mountings came later), and a host of gadgets and items of novel equipment which were sharp on the palate. . . . There had been other ships, of course, in the sixteen years between; his first command had been a river gun-boat, his second a destroyer: but he had never forgotten *Marlborough*. He had kept an eye on her all the time, checking her movements as she transferred from the Home Fleet to the Mediterranean, thence to the China Station, then home again: looking up her officers in the Navy List and wondering if they were taking proper care of her: making a special trip up to Rosyth on one of his leaves, to have another look at her; and when, at the outbreak of war, he had been given command of her, it had been like coming home again, to someone dearly loved who was not yet past the honeymoon stage.

She was not, in point of fact, much of a command for a commander, even as the senior ship of an escort group, and he could have done better if he had wished. But he did not wish. Old-fashioned she might be, battered with much hard driving, none too comfortable, at least three knots slower than the job really demanded; but she could still show her teeth and she still ran as sweet as a sewing machine, and the last three years had been the happiest of his career. He was intensely jealous of her efficiency when contrasted with more up-to-date ships, and he went to endless trouble over this, intriguing for the fitting of new equipment "for experimental purposes," demanding the replacement of officers or key-ratings if any weak point in the team began to show itself. In three years of North Atlantic convoy work he had spared neither himself nor his ship's company any of the intense strain which the job imposed; but *Marlborough* he had nursed continuously, so that the prodigious record of hours steamed and miles covered had cost the minimum of wear.

He knew her from end to end, not only with the efficient "technical" eye of the man who had watched the last five months of her building, but with an added, intimate regard for every part of her, a loving admiration, an eye tenderly blind to her short-comings.

Now she was going. No wonder he could not phrase that final order, no wonder he stared back almost angrily at the Chief, delaying what he knew must happen, waiting for the miracle to forestall it.

Up to the bridge came a new, curious noise. It came from deep within the fo'c'sle, a blend of thud and iron clang which coincided with the ship's rolling. Something very solid must have broken adrift down there, either through the shock or the unusual level of their trim, and was now washing to and fro out of control. Chief, his face puckered, tried to place it; it might have been any one of a dozen bits of heavy equipment in the forward store. The big portable pump, most likely. There must be the hell of a mess down there. Men and gear smashing up together—it hardly bore thinking of. And the noise was unnerving; it sounded like the toll of a bell, half sunk, tied to a wreck and washing with the tide. A damned sight too appropriate.

The Captain said suddenly: "I'll come down and look at that bulkhead, Chief. Haines, take over here." He turned to Adams. "You come with me. Bring one of the quartermasters, too."

There might be some piping to do in a hurry.

The journey down, deck by deck, had the same element of compulsion in it as, in a nightmare, distinguishes the random lunatic journey which can only lead to some inescapable horror at its end. The boat deck was crowded:

two loaded stretchers lay near the whaler, the figures on them not more than vague impressions of pain in the gloom: Merrett was directing the unlashing of a raft nearby: on the lee side of the funnel a dozen hands, staring out at the water, were singing "Home on the Range," in low-pitched chorus. The small party—Captain, Chief, Adams, the quartermaster—made their way aft, past the figures grouped round "X" gun, and down another ladder. At the iron-deck level, a few feet from the water, all was deserted. "I sent the damage-control party up, as soon as we'd finished, sir," the Chief said, as he stepped through the canvas screen into the alley-way leading forward. "There was nothing else for them to do."

Under cover now, the four of them moved along the rocking passage: Chief's torch picking out the way, flicking from side to side of the hollow tunnel against which the water was already lapping. Under their stumbling scraping feet the slope led fatally downwards. The clanging toll seemed to advance to meet them. They passed the entrance to the engine-room: just within, feet straddled on the grating, stood a young stocker, the link with the outside world in case the bridge voice-pipe failed. To him, as they passed, the Chief said: "No orders yet. I'll be coming back in a minute," and the stoker drew back into the shadows to pass the message on. Then they came to a closed watertight door, and this they eased slowly open, a clip at a time, so that any pressure of water within would show immediately. But it was still dry . . . the door swung back, and they stepped inside the last watertight space that lay between floating and sinking.

It was dimly lit, by two battery lanterns clipped to overhead brackets: the light struck down on a tangle of joists and beams, heel-pieces, wedges, cross-battens—the work of the damage-control party. The deck was wet underfoot, and as *Marlborough* rolled some inches of dirty water slopped from side to side, carrying with it a scummy flotsam of caps, boots, and ditty-boxes. The Captain switched on his torch, ducked under a transverse beam, and stepped up close to the bulkhead. It was, as Chief had said, in bad shape; bulging towards him, strained and leaking all down one seam, responding to the ship's movements with a long drawn-out, harsh creaking. For a single moment, as he watched it, he seemed to be looking through into the space beyond, where Number One and his fourteen damage-control hands had been caught: the forbidden picture—forbidden in the strict scheme of his captaincy—gave place to another one, conjured up in its turn by the clanging which now sounded desperately loud and clear: the three flooded mess-decks underneath his feet, the sealed-off shambles of the explosion area. Then his mind swung back, guiltily, to the only part of it that mattered now, the shored-up section he was standing in, and he nodded to himself as he glanced round it once more. It confirmed what he had been expecting but had only now faced fairly and squarely: Chief had done a good job, but it just wasn't good enough.

He turned quickly. "All right, Chief. Bring your engine-room party out on to the upper deck. Adams! Pipe 'Hands to stations for—'"

The words "Abandon ship" were cut off by a violent explosion above their heads.

For a moment the noise was so puzzling that he could not assign it to anything: it was just an interruption, almost super-natural, which had stopped him finishing that hated sentence. Then another piece of the pattern clicked into place, and he said: "That was a shell, by God!" and made swiftly for the doorway.

Outside, he called back over his shoulder: "Chief—see to the door again!" and then started to run. His footsteps rang in the confined space: he heard Adams following close behind him down the passageway, the noise echoing and clattering all round him, urging him on. Reaching the open air at last was like escaping from a nightmare into a sweating wakefulness which must somehow be instantly coordinated and controlled. As he went up the ladder to the boat-deck there was a brilliant flash and another explosion up on the bridge, followed by the sharp reek of the shell-burst. Damned good shooting from somewhere . . . something shot past his head and spun into a ventilator with a loud clang. He began to run again, brushing close by a figure making for "X" gun shouting "Close up again! Load starshell!" Guns, at least, had his part of it under control.

He passed the space between the two boats. It was here, he saw, that the first shell had struck: the motor-boat was damaged, one of the stretchers was overturned, and there were three separate groups of men bending over figures stretched out on deck. He wanted to stop and find out how bad the damage was, and, especially, how many men had been killed or hurt, but he could not: the bridge called him, and had the prior claim.

It was while he was climbing quickly up the ladder that he realized that the moon had now risen, low in the sky, and the *Marlborough* must be cleanly silhouetted against the horizon. If no one on the upper deck had seen the flash of the submarine's firing, the moon ought to give them a line on her position. Guns would probably work that out for himself. But it would be better to make sure.

Now he was at the top of the ladder, his eyes grown accustomed to the gloom, his nostrils assailed by the acrid stink of the explosion. The shell he had seen land when he first came out on deck had caught the bridge fair and square, going through one wing and exploding against the chart-house. Only two men were still on their feet—the signalman and one of the look-outs: the other look-out was lying, headless, against his machine-gun mounting. Adams, at his shoulder, drew in his breath sharply at the sight, but the Captain's eyes had already moved farther on, to where three other figures—who must be Haines, the midshipman, and the messenger—had fallen in a curiously theatrical grouping round the compass platform. The light there was too dim to show any details: the dark shambles could only be guessed at. But one of the figures was still moving. It was the midshipman, clinging to a voice-pipe and trying to hoist himself upright.

He said quickly: "Lie still, Mid.," and then: "Signalman, give me the hailer," and lastly, to Adams: "Do what you can for them." He caught sight of the young, shocked face of the other look-out staring at him, and he called out sharply: "Don't look inboard. Watch your proper arc. Use your glasses." Then he switched on the microphone, and spoke into it:

" 'X' gun, 'X' gun—illuminate away from the moon—illuminate away from the moon." He paused, then continued: "Doctor or sick-berth attendant report to the bridge now—doctor or sick-berth attendant."

Pity had inclined him to put the last order first: the instinct of command had told him otherwise. But almost before he stopped speaking, the sharp crack of "X" gun came from aft, and the star-shell soared. Guns had had the same idea as himself.

Adams, who was kneeling down and working away at a rough tourniquet, said over his shoulder:

"Shall I carry on with that pipe, sir?"

"No. Wait."

The U-boat coming to the surface had altered everything. The ship was now only a platform for "X" gun, and not to be abandoned while "X" gun still had work to do.

As the star-shell burst and hung, lighting up the grey moving sea, the Captain raised his glasses and swept the arc of water that lay on their beam. Almost immediately he saw the U-boat, stopped on the surface, broadside on to them and not more than a mile away. Before he had time to speak over the hailer, or give any warning, there was a noise from aft as Guns shouted a fresh order; and then things happened very quickly.

"X" gun roared. A spout of water, luminous under the star-shell, leapt upwards, just beyond the U-boat and dead in line—a superb sighting shot, considering the suddenness of this new crisis. There was a pause, while the

Captain's mind raced over the two possibilities now open—that the U-boat, guessing she had only a badly crippled ship to deal with, would fight it out on the surface, or that she would submerge to periscope depth and fire another torpedo. Then came the next shot, to settle all his doubts.

It came from both ships, and it was almost farcically conclusive. The flash of both guns was instantaneous. The U-boat's shell exploded aft, right on "X" gun, ripping the whole platform to pieces; but from the U-boat herself a brilliant orange flash spurted suddenly, to be succeeded by the crump of an explosion. Then she disappeared completely.

"X" gun, mortally wounded itself, had made its last shot a mortal one for the enemy.

Silence now over all the ship, save for a faint moaning from aft. The Captain reached for the hailer, and then paused. No point in saying anything at this moment: they would be looking after "X" gun's crew, what was left of them, and there was no more enemy to deal with. He listened for a moment to Adams's heavy breathing as he bent over the midshipman, and then turned as a figure showed itself at the top of the bridge-ladder.

"Captain, sir."

"What is it?"

"S.B.A., sir. The doctor's gone aft to the gun."

"All right. Bear a hand here. Who's that behind you?"

"It's me, sir," said Bridger's voice from the top of the ladder. "I was helping the S.B.A."

"Were you up here when the second shell landed?"

"No, sir—just missed it." Bridger sounded competent and unsurprised, as if he had arranged the thing that way. "I went down to give them a hand when the first one hit the boat-deck, sir."

"How much damage down there?"

"Killed three of the lads, sir." The sick-berth attendant's voice breaking in was strained and rather uneven. "Mr. Merrett's gone, too. He was just by the motor-boat."

Another officer lost. Guns had probably been killed, too. That meant—the Captain checked suddenly, running over the list in his mind. Number One, caught by the bulkhead. Haines and the midshipman finished up here; Merrett gone, dying typically in a quiet corner, escaping his notice. Guns almost certainly killed at "X" gun. That meant that there were no executive officers left at all: only Chief and the doctor. If they didn't abandon ship—if somehow they got her going again—it would be an almost impossible job, single-handed. . . . He put the thought on one side for the moment, and said to the sick-berth attendant:

"Take over from Petty Officer Adams. Have a look at the others first, and then get the midshipman aft to the wardroom."

He waited again, as the man got to work. The heavy clanging from below, which had stopped momentarily when the gun was fired, now started once more. Presently the doctor came up to the bridge, to report what he had been expecting to hear—that Guns, and the whole crew of seven, had been killed by the last shot from the U-boat. Even though he had been prepared for it, it was impossible to hear the news with indifference. But for some reason it confirmed a thought which had been growing in his mind, ever since the U-boat had been sunk. They were on their own now, and the only danger was from the sea. His loved *Marlborough* had survived so much, had produced such a brilliant last-minute counterstroke, that he could not leave her now. Reason told him to carry on with the order he had given down below, but reason seemed to have had no part in the last few minutes: something else, some product of heart and instinct, seemed to have taken control of them all. That last shot of "X" gun had been a miracle. Suppose there were more miracles on the way?

Adams, straightening up as the sick-berth attendant took over, once again tried, respectfully, to recall the critical moment to him:

"Carry on with that pipe, sir?"

"No." The Captain, divining the uncertainty in the man's mind, smiled in the darkness. "No, Adams, I hadn't forgotten. But we'll wait till daylight."

Chapter Two

~~~~~~~~~~~~~~~~~~~~~~~~~~~~~~~~~~

THERE were fourteen hours till daylight: fourteen hours to review that decision, to ascribe it correctly either to emotion or to a reasonable assessment of chance, and to foresee the outcome. What struck the Captain most strongly about it was the unprofessional aspect of what he had done. Down there in the shored-up fo'c'sle, he had made a precise, technical examination of the damage and the repairs to it, and come to a clear decision: if the U-boat's shell had not hit them, and interrupted the order, they would now be sitting in the boats, lying off in the darkness and waiting for *Marlborough* to go down. But something had intervened: not simply the absolute necessity of fighting the U-boat as long as possible, not even second thoughts on their chance of keeping the ship afloat, but something stronger still. It was so long since the Captain had changed his mind about any personal or professional decision that he hardly knew how to analyse it. But certainly the change of mind was there.

He could find excuses for it now, though not very adequate ones. Daylight would give them more chance to survey the damage properly. (But he had done that already.) With the motor-boat wrecked by the first shell-burst, there were not enough boats for the crew to take to. (But some of them would always have to use rafts anyway, and if *Marlborough* sank they would have no choice in the matter.) They had a number of badly wounded men on board who must be sheltered for as long as possible, if they were not to die of neglect or exposure. (But they certainly stood more chance of surviving an orderly abandonment of the ship, rather than a last-minute emergency retreat.) No, none of these ideas had really any part in it. It boiled down to nothing more precise than a surge of feeling which had attacked him as soon as the U-boat was sunk: a foolish emotional idea, product both of the past years and of this last tremendous stroke, that after *Marlborough* had done so much for them they could not leave her to die. It wasn't an explanation which would look well in the Report of Proceedings; but it was as near the truth as he could phrase it.

The answer would come with daylight, anyway: till then he must wait. If the bulkhead held, and the weather moderated, and Chief was able to get things going again (that main switchboard would have to be rewired, for a start), then they might be able to do something: creep southwards, perhaps, till they were athwart the main convoy route and could get help. It was the longest chance he had ever taken: sitting there in his chair up on the bridge, brooding in the darkness, he tried to visualize its successive stages. Funnier things had happened at sea. . . . But the final picture, the one that remained with him all that night, was of a ship—his ship—drawing thirty-two feet forward and nothing aft, drifting helplessly down wind with little prospect of surviving till daylight.

No one ashore knew anything about them,

and no one would start worrying for at least three days.

Within the ship, ignoring and somehow isolating itself against this preposterous weight of odds, there was much to do; and with no officers to call on except the doctor, who was busy with casualties, and the Chief, whom he left to make a start in the engine-room, the Captain set to work to organize it himself. He kept Bridger by him, to relay orders, and a signalman, in case something unexpected happend (there was a faint chance of an aircraft on passage being in their area, and within signalling distance): Adams was installed as a virtual First Lieutenant; and from this nucleus the control and routine of the ship was set in motion again.

The bulkhead he could do nothing about: Chief set to work on the main switchboard, the first step towards raising steam again, and the leading telegraphist was working on the wireless transmitter; the boats and rafts were left in instant readiness, and the more severe casualties taken back under cover again. (A hard decision, this; but to keep them on the upper deck in this bitter weather was a degree nearer killing them than running the risk of trapping them below.) Among the casualties was the midshipman, still alive after a cruel lacerated wound in the chest and now in the sick-bay waiting for a blood transfusion. The bodies of the other three who had been killed on the bridge—Haines, the lookout, and the bridge messenger—had been taken aft to the quarterdeck, to join the rest, from "X" gun's crew and the party on the boat-deck, awaiting burial.

Then, after a spell of cleaning up, which included the chaos of loose gear and ammunition round "A" gun, which had been directly over the explosion, the Captain told Adams to muster what was left of the ship's company and report the numbers. He was still in his chair on the bridge, sipping a mug of cocoa, which Bridger had cooked up in the ward-room pantry, when Adams came up with his report, and he listened to the details with an attention which he tried to rid of all personal feeling. These crude figures, which Adams, bending over the chart-table light, was reading out, were men, some of them well known and liked, some of them shipmates of two and three years' standing, all of them sailors; but from now on they must only be numbers, only losses on a chart of activity and endurance. The dead were not to be sailors any more: just "missing potential," "negative assets"—some damned phrase like that.

Adams said: "I've written it all down, sir, as well as I could." He had, in his voice, the same matter-of-fact impersonal tone as the Captain would have used: the words "as well as I could" might have referred to some trifling clerical inconvenience instead of the difficulty of sorting out the living, the dead, and the dying in the pitch darkness. "There's the ones we know about, first. There's three officers and twelve ratings killed—that's the Gunnery Officer, Lieutenant Haines, and Mr. Merrett, and the gun's crew and the ones on the boat-deck and the two up here. The surgeon-lieutenant has one officer and sixteen men in the sick-bay. We'll have to count most of them out, I'm afraid, sir. Nine of them were out of the fo'c'sle. Then there's"—he paused—"one officer and seventy-four men missing." He stopped again, expecting the Captain to say something, but as no word came from the dark figure in the chair he went on: "Then what we've got left sir. There's yourself, and the surgeon-lieutenant, and the engineer—

that's three officers, and twenty-eight men out of the Red Watch, the one that was on duty."

"Twenty-eight. Is that all?"

"That's all, sir. They lost seven seamen at 'X' gun, three by the boats, and two here. Then there's seven of them down in the sickbay. That's forty-seven altogether."

"How are the twenty-eight made up? How many seaman have we?"

Adams straightened up and turned round from the table. This part of it he evidently knew by heart. "There's myself, sir, and Leading Seaman Tapper, and seven A.B.'s: the quartermaster and the bosun's mate, that were in the wheel-house: and Bridger. That's twelve. Then there's the hands who were on watch in the W/T office: the leading tel. and two others, and two coders. That makes seventeen altogether. The signalman up here, eighteen. The S.B.A., nineteen. The leading steward, twenty."

"Any other stewards?"

"No, sir."

It didn't matter, thought the Captain: no officers, either.

"The rest were all engine-room branch,

sir," Adams went on. "Eight of them altogether."

"How are they made up?"

"It's pretty good, sir, as far as experience
goes. The Chief E.R.A. and one of the younger
ones, and a stoker petty officer and five stokers.
If it was just one watch they'd be all right.
But of course there's no reliefs for them, and
they'll have to be split into two watches if it
comes to steaming." Adams paused, on the
verge of a question, but the Captain, seeing
it coming, interrupted him. He didn't yet feel
ready to discuss their chances of getting under
way again.

"Just give me those figures again, Adams,"
he said, "as I say the headings. Let's have the
fit men first."

Adams bent down to the light once more.
"Yourself and two officers and twenty-eight
men, sir."

"Killed and wounded?"

Adams added quickly: "Four officers and
twenty-eight."

"And missing, the First Lieutenant and
seventy-four." He had no need to be reminded
of that item: that "seventy-four" would stay
with him always. Not counting the accident to

Number One's damage-control party, there must have been sixty men killed or cut off by the first explosion. All of them still there, deep down underneath his feet. Twenty-eight left out of a hundred and thirty. Whatever he was able to do with the *Marlborough* now, the weight of those figures could never be lightened.

"Will I make some more cocoa, sir?" said Bridger suddenly. He had been waiting in silence all this time, standing behind the Captain's chair. The numbers and details which Adams had produced, even though they concerned Bridger's own mess mates, were real to him only so far as they affected the Captain: this moment, he judged instinctively, was the worst so far, and he tried to dissipate it in the only way open to him.

The Captain's figure, which had been hunched deep in the chair, straightened suddenly. He shook himself. The cold air was stiffening his legs, and he stood up. "No, thanks, Bridger," he answered. "I'm going to turn in, in a minute. Bring up my sleeping-bag and a pillow, and I'll sleep in the asdic hut."

"Aye, aye, sir." Bridger clumped off at a

solid workmanlike pace, his heavy sea-boots ringing their way down the ladder. The Captain turned to Adams again. "We'd better work out a routine for the time between now and daylight," he said briskly. "We can leave the engine-room out of it for the moment: they're busy enough. You'd better arrange the seamen in two watches: the telegraphists and coders can work in with them, except for the leading tel.—he can stay on the set. Send half the hands off watch now: they can sleep in the wardroom alley way or on the upper deck, whichever they prefer. The rest can carry on with cleaning up."

"The doctor may want some help down there, sir."

"Yes—see about that too. . . . Keep two lookouts on the upper deck for the rest of to-night: tell them they're listening for aircraft as well. We'll show an Aldis lamp if we hear anything, and chance it being hostile. You'd better put the signalman up here, with those instructions; and pick out the most intelligent coder, and have him work watch-and-watch with the signalman. That's about all, I think. See that I'm called if anything happens."

"Do you want a hand to watch that bulk-head, sir?"

"No. The engine-room will cover that: they're nearest. About meals. . . ." The Captain scratched his chin. "We'll just have to do our best with the wardroom pantry. There were some dry provisions in the after store, weren't there?"

"Corned beef and biscuits, sir, and some tinned milk, I think. And there's plenty of tea. We'll not go short."

"Right. . . . That'll do for to-night, then. I'll see what things are like in the morning: there'll be plenty of squaring up to do. You'll have to get those bodies sewn up, too. If we do get under way again," the Captain tried, and failed, to say this in a normal voice, "you'll have to work out a scheme of guns' crews and look-outs and quartermasters."

"Better take the wheel myself, sir."

The Captain smiled. "It won't exactly be fleet manoeuvres, Adams."

The expected question came last. "How much chance have we got, sir?"

"Hard to say." He answered it as unemotionally as he could. "You saw the state that bulkhead was in. It might go any time, or it might hold indefinitely. But even very slow headway would make a big difference to the strain on it, unless the bows stay rigid where they are, and take most of the weight. Almost everything depends on the weather."

As he said this, the arrangements he had been making with Adams receded into the background, and he became aware of the ship again, and of her sluggish motion under his feet. She was quieter now, certainly: no shocks or grinding from below, no advertisement of distress. But he could feel, as if it were going on inside his own body, the strain on the whole ship, the anguish of that slow cumbersome roll down wind. Earlier she had seemed to be dying: this now was the rallying process, infinitely painful both to endure and to watch. Long after Adams had left the bridge, the Captain still stood there, suffering all that the ship suffered, aware that the only effective anaesthetic was death.

It was an idea which at any other time he would have dismissed as fanciful and ridiculous, unseamanlike as a poet talking of his soul. Now it was natural, deeply felt and deeply resented. His professional responsibility for *Marlborough* was transformed: he felt for her nothing save anger and pity.

Just before he turned in, Chief came up from below to report progress. He stood at the top of the ladder, a tired but not dissipirited figure, and his voice had the old downright confidence on which the Captain had come to rely. He had been in *Marlborough* for nearly three years; as an engineering lieutenant he, too, could probably have got a better job, but he had never shown any signs of wanting one.

"We've made a good start on the switch-board, sir," he began. "We ought to get the fans going some time to-morrow." There was nothing in his tone to suggest the danger, which he must have felt all the time, of working deep down below decks at a time like this. "The boiler-room's in a bit of a mess—there's a lot of water about—but we'll clear that up as soon as we can get pressure on the pumps."

"What about the bulkhead, Chief?"

"It's about the same, sir. I've been in once myself, and I've a hand listening all the time outside the next watertight door. There's nothing to report there." He turned, and looked behind him down the length of the ship, and then up at the sky. "She seems a lot easier, sir."

"Yes, the wind's going down." The phrase was like a blessing.

"By God, we'll do it yet!" Chief, preparing to go down again, slurred his feet along the deck and found it sticky. "Bit of a mess here," he commented.

"Blood," said the Captain shortly. "They haven't cleaned up yet."

"We're going to be pretty shorthanded," said the Chief, following a natural train of thought. "But that's to-morrow's worry. Good night, sir."

"Good night, Chief. Get some sleep if you can."

But later he himself found sleep almost impossible to achieve, weary as he was after nearly nine hours on the bridge. He lay in his sleeping-bag on the hard floor of the asdic hut, feeling underneath him the trials and tremors of the ship's painful labouring. It was very cold. Poor *Marlborough,* he thought, losing between waking and sleeping the full control of his thoughts. Poor old *Marlborough.* We shouldn't do this to you. None of us should: not us, or the Germans, or those poor chaps washing about in the fo'c'sle. No ship deserved an ordeal as evil as this. Only human beings, immeasurably base, deserved such punishment.

Bridger woke him at first light, with a mug of tea and an insinuating "Seven o'clock, sir!" so normal as to make him smile. But the smile was not much more than a momentary flicker. Under him he felt the ship very slowly rolling to and fro, without will and without protest: she seemed more a part of the sea itself than a separate burden on it. The weather must have moderated a lot, but *Marlborough* might be deeper in the water as well.

Cold and stiff, he lay for a few minutes before getting up, collecting his thoughts and remembering what was waiting for him outside the asdic hut. It would be bitterly cold, possibly wet as well: the ship would seem deformed and ugly, the damage meeting his eyes at every turn: the blood on the bridge would be dried black. All over the upper deck there would be men, grey-faced and shivering, waking to face the day: not cheerful and noisy as they usually were, but dully astonished that the ship was still afloat and that they had survived so far; unwilling, even, to meet each other's eye, in the embarrassment of fear and disbelief of the future. And there were those other men down in the fo'c'sle, who would not wake. There were the burials to see to. There was the bulkhead.

He got up.

The bulkhead first, with the Chief and Adams. The rating outside the water-tight door said: "Haven't heard anything, sir," in a noncommittal way, as if he did not really believe that they were not all wasting their time. He was a young stoker: sixteen men in his mess had been caught forward: no hope of any sort had yet been communicated to him. Noting this, the Captain thought: I'll have to talk to them, some time this morning. . . . Inside, things were as before: there was a little more water, and the atmosphere was now thick and sour: but nothing had shifted, and with the decrease in the ship's rolling the bulkhead itself was rigid, without sound or movement.

"I think it's even improved a bit, sir," said the Chief. He ran his hand down the central seam, which before had been leaking: his fingers now came away dry. "This seems to have worked itself watertight again. If we could alter the trim a bit, so that even part of this space is above the water-line, we might be able to save it."

"That's going to be to-day's job," said the Captain, "moving everything we can aft, so as to bring her head up a bit. I'll go into details when we get outside."

On his way back he visited the boiler- and engine- rooms. The boiler-room was deserted, and already cooling fast: here again the forward bulkhead was a tangle of shores and joists, braced against the angle-pieces that joined the frames.

"What about this one?" he asked.

"Doesn't seem to be any strain on it, sir," Chief answered. "I think the space next to it—that's the drying-room and the small bosun's store—must still be watertight."

The Captain nodded without saying anything. He was begining to feel immensely and unreasonably cheerful, but to communicate that feeling to anyone else seemed frivolous in the extreme. There was so little to go on: it might all be a product of what he felt about the ship herself, and unfit to be shared with anyone.

The engine-room was very much alive. Two men—the Chief E.R.A. and a young telegraphist—were working on the main switchboard: the telegraphist, lying flat on his back behind it, was pulling through a length of thick insulated cable and connecting it up. Two more hands were busy on one of the main steam valves. There was an air of purpose here, of men who knew clearly what the next job was to be, and how to set about it.

The Chief E.R.A., an old pensioner with a smooth bald head in odd contrast with the craggy wrinkles of his face, smiled when he saw the Captain. They came from the same Kentish village, and the Chief E.R.A.'s appointment to *Marlborough* had been the biggest wangle the Captain had ever undertaken. But it had been justified a score of times in the last two years, and obviously it was in process of being justified again now.

"Well, Chief?"

"Going on all right, sir. It won't be much to look at, but I reckon it'll serve."

"That's all we want." The Captain turned to the engineer officer. "Any other troubles down here?"

"I'm a bit worried about the port engine, sir. That torpedo was a big shock. It may have knocked the shaft out."

"It doesn't matter if we only have one screw. We couldn't go more than a few knots anyway, with that bulkhead."

"That's what I thought, sir."

The Chief E.R.A., presuming on their peacetime friendship in a way which the Captain had anticipated, and did not mind, said:

"Do you think we'll be able to steam, sir?"

Everyone in the engine-room stopped work to listen to the answer. The Captain hesitated a moment, and then said:

"If the weather stays like it is now, and we can correct the trim a bit, I think we ought to make a start."

"How far to go, sir?"

"About five hundred miles." That was as much as he wanted to talk about it and he nodded and turned to go. With his foot on the ladder he said: "I expect we'll be able to count every one of them."

The laughter as he began to climb was a tonic for himself as well. It hadn't been a very good joke, but it was the first one for a long time.

The sick-bay next. The doctor was asleep in an arm-chair when he came in, his young sensitive face turned away from the light, his hands splayed out on the arms of the chair as if each individual finger were resting after an exhaustive effort. The sick-berth attendant was bending over one of the lower cots, where a bandaged figure lay with closed, deeply circled eyes. There were eight men altogether: after the night's turmoil the room was surprisingly tidy, save for a pile of blood-stained swabs and dressings which had overflowed from the wastebasket. The tidiness and the sharp aseptic smell were reassuring.

He put his hand out, and touched the sleeping figure.

"Good morning, Doctor."

Soundlessly the doctor woke, opened his eyes, and sat up. Even this movement seemed part of some controlled competent routine.

"Hallo, sir!"

"Busy night?"

"Very, sir. All right, though."

"Just what you were waiting for?" The Captain smiled.

The doctor looked at the Captain, and smiled back, and said: "I haven't felt so well for years."

It must be odd to feel like that, about what must surely have been the goriest night of his life. But it was natural, if you were proud and confident of your professional skill, and for three years you felt you had been utterly wasted. This young man, who had barely been qualified when war broke out, must now feel, with justice, that the initials after his name had at last come to life.

The Captain looked round the sick-bay. "Where are the rest of them? Adams said you had sixteen."

"Four died." It was extraordinary how the simplicity of phrase and tone still conveyed an assurance that the lives had been fought for, and only surrendered in the last extremity. "I've spread the rest over the officers' cabins, where they'll be more comfortable. There's one in yours, sir."

"That's all right. . . . How's the midshipman?"

"Bad. In fact going, I'm afraid, sir. That chest wound was too deep, and he lost too much blood. Do you want to take a look at him? He's in his own cabin."

"Is he conscious?"

The doctor shook his head. "No. I've had to dope him pretty thoroughly. That's the trouble: if I go on doping him he'll die of it, and if I let him wake up there's enough shock and pain to kill him almost immediately. That's why it's no good." Again the simple tone seemed able to imply an infinity of skill and care, which had proved unavailing.

"I won't bother, then." The phrase sounded callous, but he did not bother to qualify it: he was suddenly impatient to leave this antiseptic corner, and get to work on the ship. She, at least, was still among the living: no dope, no ordered death-bed for her. He had skill and care of his own sort. . . .

As he came out on the quarterdeck he checked his step, for there, arranged in neat rows, which somehow seemed a caricature of the whole idea of burial, were the sewn-up bodies which he must later commit to the deep. Nineteen of them: three officers and sixteen men. There had not been enough ensigns to cover them all, he noted: here and there three of them shared one flag, crowding under it in a pathetic, last-minute symbolism. . . . Adams, who had been waiting for him, straightened up as he emerged. He had only been bending down to adjust one of the formal canvas packages; but the Captain had a sudden ghoulish fancy that Adams had been giving it the traditional "last stitch"—the needle and thread through the nose, by which the sailmaker used to satisfy himself that the body he was sewing up was beyond doubt that of a dead man. The Captain looked away, and up at the sky. It was full light now: a grey cold day, the veiled sun shedding the thinnest watery gleam, the waste of water round them reduced to a long flat swell. The passing of the storm, or some lull in its centre, had brought a windless day for their respite.

Chief, who had waited behind in the engine-room, now joined them, and together the three men crossed the upper deck towards the fo'c'sle. The Captain led the party, picking his way past the bloody ruin of "X" gun, and the men who were at work cleaning up. He was conscious of them looking at him: conscious of a suppressed, heightened tension among them all: conscious, for example, that Leading Seaman Tapper, not an outstanding personality, had this morning assumed a new, almost heroic bearing. As the only leading seaman left alive, he was already rising to the challenge. . . . With the coming of daylight all these men had won back what the stoker, working and waiting below decks, still lacked: hope in the future, confidence in themselves and the ship. "The ship is your best lifebelt"—a phrase in his Standing Orders for damage-control returned to him. By God, that was still true; and all the men up here trusted and believed it.

Presently they were standing on the fo'c'sle by "A" gun. From here the deck, buckled and distorted, led steeply downwards, till the bull-ring in the bows was not more than three or four feet from the water: even allowing for this downward curve of the deck, *Marlborough* must be drawing about twenty-eight feet instead of her normal sixteen. Obviously, the first essential was to correct this if possible: not only to ease the pressure forward when they started moving, but also to bring the screws fully under water again.

The Captain stepped forward carefully till he was standing directly over the explosion area: there he leant over the rail, staring down into the water a few feet away. From somewhere below an oily scum oozed out, trailing aft and away like some disgusting suppuration; but of the wound itself nothing could be seen. Unprofessionally, he was glad of that: it was sufficiently distressing to note the broad outlines of *Marlborough's* plight on this cold grey morning, without being confronted with the gross details. He realized suddenly that this must now be treated as a technical problem, and nothing more, and after a quick look round the rest of the fo'c'sle he turned back to the Chief and Adams.

"I've got three ideas," he said briskly. "You may have some more. . . . For a start, we'll get rid of as much as possible of this"—he tapped one of the lowered barrels of "A" gun, askew on its drooping platform. "It wouldn't be safe to fire them anyway, so we can ditch the barrels—and even the mounting itself if we can lift it clear."

"The derrick can deal with the barrels, sir," said Adams. "I don't know about the rest."

"We'll see. . . . Then there are the anchors. We can either let them run out altogether, with their cables, or else let the anchors go by themselves, and manhandle the cable aft as a counterweight. What do you think, Chief?"

"The second idea is the best one, sir. But without steam on the windlass we can't get the cable out of the locker."

"We'll have to do that by hand." The Captain turned to Adams again. "We've still got one of those weapons, haven't we?—the ratchet-and-pawl lever?"

"Yes, sir. It's a long job, though."

"I know." They had once had to weigh anchor by this archaic method, a long time ago, bringing in the cable link by link, half a link to each stroke of the lever, which needed four men to operate it. It had been an agonizingly slow process, taking nearly six hours and everyone's temper. Now they would have to do it to each cable in turn. . . . "But it's worth it, to get some of the weight aft. Then there's the windlass itself. If we pull it to pieces and use a sheer-legs to lift the heavy parts, we might get rid of a lot of weight that way."

The Engineer Officer nodded, rather abstractedly. It would be his job later to account for all this, item by item, in triplicate at least, and the whole thing was a horrid distortion of the principles of storekeeping. But he put the thought on one side, and produced an idea which must have been professionally more acceptable.

"I was wondering about the fore-peak, sir," he began. "You know we've kept it flooded for the last two trips, to balance the weight of those extra depth-charges aft. We can't pump it out now, because the suction-line is broken. But if we took this cover-plate off"— he pointed to the small plate screwed to the deck, right up in the bows—"and made sure the compartment was still isolated, we could pump it out by hand. That would give us some buoyancy just where we need it."

The Captain nodded quickly. "Good idea, Chief. "You'll have to go carefully, though, in case the bulkhead's gone and it's all part of the explosion area. By the way, what's the fuel situation going to be, with all this part isolated?"

"Oh, we'll have plenty, sir, especially if we're only steaming on one boiler. We've still got the two big tanks aft."

"Right. . . ." He looked out at the sea again, and then at his watch. It was nearly nine. "I'll read the burial service in half an hour, Adams, if you'll have everything ready by then. Then you can make a start on the weight-lifting programme—the gun first, and then the anchors. Can you spare any stokers, Chief?"

"Maybe two, sir."

"The fresh air will be a nice change for them. . . ."

His spirits were rising.

But there was nothing artificial, no formal assumption of mourning, in what he felt half an hour later, as he opened his prayer book, gave "Off caps" in a low, almost gentle voice, and prepared to read the service. All that remained of his ship's company stood in a rough square on the quarterdeck: at their feet the nineteen bodies, in their canvas shrouds, seemed like some sinister carpet from which they could not take their eyes. There were altogether too many of them: barely did the living outnumber the dead, and if the men caught in the fo'c'sle were reckoned the living were only curious survivals of a vanished time. . . . That pause in the service, when he said "We do now commit their bodies to the deep," and then waited, as the burial party got to work and the nineteen bodies made their successive splashes, their long dive—that pause seemed to be lasting for ever.

The men in their stained sea-boots and duffle coats stood silent, their hair ruffled, watching the bodies go: flanking him, the doctor and the Chief completed the square of witnesses. The rough canvases scraped the deck as they were dragged across; the bodies splashed and vanished; the ship rolled, and all their feet shifted automatically to meet it; a seaman coughed; the silence under the cold sky was oppressive and somehow futile. He himself, with an appalling clarity of feeling, was conscious of cruel loss. These had been his own men: to see them "discharged dead" in this perfunctory wholesale fashion only deepened the sense of personal bereavement which was in his face and his voice as he took up the reading again.

When it was done he put the book away and faced his ship's company: in their expression, too, was something of the wastage and sadness of the moment. It was not what he wished to dwell on, but he could not dismiss it without a word: that would have been as cruelly artificial as using the dead men to whip up hatred, or additional energy for the task ahead. It was no time for anything save sincerity.

"I shall never need reminding of this moment," he began, "and I know that is true for all of you too. We have lost good men, good shipmates, and there are many more whom we

78

cannot even reach to give them proper burial. We can't forget them, any more than we can forget the three officers and sixteen men we've just seen over the side. But," he raised his voice a little, "one of the hardest things of war is that there is never any spare time to think about these things, or to mourn men like these as they deserve. That has to come later: there's always something to do; and in this case it's going to be the toughest job any of us has ever undertaken. I might as well tell you that I nearly gave the order to abandon ship last night: for the moment the weather has saved us, and we must do our utmost to profit by it. I'm not going to hold out too much hope: but if the weather holds, and the bulkhead, which is taking most of the strain, doesn't collapse, and if I can correct the trim, we stand a good chance of getting in—or at least of going far enough south to meet other ships." He smiled. "You can see there are a lot of 'ifs' about this job. But it would be a hundred times worth trying, even if our lives didn't depend on it. I myself am going to do my utmost to get this ship in, and I'm counting on every man to back me up. Remember there are only thirty-one of us altogether, and that means a double

and triple effort from each one of you. . . .
We'll stand easy now, and then get to work.
And keep this idea in the back of your minds:
if we do get *Marlborough* in, it will be the
finest thing any of us have ever done."

He wanted to say more: affected as he had
been by the burials, he wanted to dwell on this
aspect of sacrifice, and on *Marlborough* as a
measure of its validity and as something dear
to them all. But he was afraid of sounding
theatrical: better perhaps to leave it like this,
a challenge to their endurance and seamanship, and look to the outcome.

When he returned to the bridge he took out
the deck-log and began to make an entry con-
cerning the death and burial of his men. It
was while he was adding the nineteen names
and ratings that he noticed it was the morning
of New Year's Day.

Chapter Three

~~~~~~

ALL that day they lay there, the ship's only motion a sluggish rolling. But within her the movement and the noises were cheerful. The ditching of "A" gun barrels and the greater part of the mounting was easy: the breaking and moving of the anchor cables a long drawn-out effort which lasted till well after dark. But the cables, hauled in sections along the upper deck and stowed right aft among the depth-charges, made an appreciable difference to their trim: so did the jettisoned windlass, which disappeared overboard bit by bit, as in some mysterious conjuring trick. (It was too heavy and unwieldy to move aft.) But the pumping out of the fore-peak (the triangular section which makes up the bows) was the most successful of all. It acted as a buoyancy chamber where it could exert the most leverage, and it brought the bows up cheerfully. Altogether, by the time the programme was fulfilled, the draught forrard had improved to twenty-four feet, and the screws aft were deep enough to get a firm grip of the water. Of course, she would steer like a mongrel waving its tail; but that wouldn't matter. There was no one watching.

One curious accident attended the lightening process. As *Marlborough's* draught forrard began to alter decisively, two bodies, released by some chance movement of the hull, floated out from the hole in the port side. They drifted away before they could be recovered: they were both badly burned, and both sprawling in relaxed, ungainly attitudes as though glad to be quit of their burden. The Captain, looking down from the bridge, watched them with absorbed attention, obsessed by the fancy that they were a first instalment of the sacrifice which must be paid before the ship got under way. He heard a rating on the fo'c'sle say: "The second one was Fletcher—poor bastard," and he felt angry at the curt epitaph, as if its informality might somehow weaken the magic. He could not remember having had thoughts like that since he was a small boy. Perhaps it was the beginning of feeling really tired.

For him it had been a long day, and now at dusk, with the prospect of another night of drifting, he felt impatient to put things to the test. He had been all over the ship again: he had seen the midshipman and two ratings who were also dying: he had looked at the radio set (from which the leading tel. had at last stood back and said: "It's no good, sir—there's too much smashed"): he had made a third examination of the bulkhead, where they had been able to insert another shore and a felt-and-tallow patch, to take up the slack as the pressure on it relaxed. He had directed the work on the cables, Adams being busy on "A" gun. Now he had nothing to do but wait for Chief's report from the engine-room: the hardest part of all. He had the sky to watch, and the barometer, low but steady; and that was all. The main ordeal still lay ahead.

It was nine o'clock that evening before the Engineer Officer came up with his report: the Captain was sitting in the deserted wardroom aft, eating the corned beef hash which was now their staple diet and remembering other parties which this room had witnessed, when there were eight of them, with Number One's wife and Gun's fiancée and one of the Mid.'s colourful young women to cheer them. Now the dead men and the mourning women outnumbered the living: no charm, no laughter could enliven any of the absent. . . . Impatiently he ground a half-smoked cigarette into his plate, cursing these ridiculous thoughts and fancies, unlike any he could remember, which were beginning to crowd in on him. There was no time to spare for such irrelevancies: he had one supreme task to concentrate on, and anything else was a drain on energy and attention alike.

Chief came in, shedding a pair of oily gauntlets, looking down apologetically at his stained white overalls.

"Well, Chief?"

"Pretty good, sir." He crossed to the pantry hatch and hammered on it, demanding his supper. Then he sat down in his usual place at the foot of the table, and leant back. "The switchboard's done, and they're working on the dynamo now: it had a bad shake up, but

I think we'll manage." He was obviously very tired, eyelids drooping in a grey lined face. The Captain suddenly realized how much depended on this man's skill. "I'll be flashing up when I've finished supper."

"How long before we can steam?"

"Can't say to the nearest hour, sir. It'll be some time to-morrow, unless we run into more snags. There's the boiler room to pump out, and a lot of cleaning up besides. It'll only be one screw, I'm afraid. The other's nearly locked: the shaft must be badly bent."

"It doesn't matter."

Bridger came in with the Chief's supper, and for a little while there was silence as he ate. Then, between bites, he asked:

"How the midshipman, sir?"

"Pretty nearly gone. God knows what keeps him alive. His chest's in an awful mess."

Chief looked round the room, and said: "It's funny to see this place empty."

There was silence again till he had finished eating. They shared the same thoughts, but it was less discomforting to leave them unspoken. Bridger, coming in with the Chief's coffee, broke the silence by asking the Captain:

"Will you be sleeping down here, sir?"

"No, in the asdic hut again."

"Will you see Petty Officer Adams, sir?"

"Yes. Tell him to come in."

There was a whispering in the pantry, and Adams came in, cap in hand. Same routine to-night, sir?" he asked.

"Yes, Adams. Two look-outs and the signalman on the bridge. I'll be in the asdic hut."

"Aye, aye, sir."

"Things seem to be going all right. We should get going some time to-morrow."

Adam's severe face cracked into a grin. "Can I tell the hands, sir?"

"Yes, do." The Captain stood up, and began to put on his duffle coat. "How about some sleep for you, Chief?"

The Chief nodded. "As soon as I've finished up, sir. There'll be a bit of time to spare them." Relaxing, with coffee cup in hand, he looked round the wardroom. "New Year's Day. I wish we had the radio. It feels so cut off."

"With luck you'll have your bedtime music tomorrow." He went out, stepping over the dozen sleeping men who crowded the alley way, and made his way forward to the bridge again. With luck to-morrow might bring everything they were waiting for.

The sea was still calm, the glass unwaveringly steady.

He awoke suddenly at five o'clock, startled and uneasy. For a moment he puzzled over what had disturbed him: then he realized gratefully what it was. The lights had come on, and the little heater screwed to the bulkhead was glowing. It meant that the dynamos were now running properly, and the switchboard, which the Chief had been reserving for the engine-room circuit, was able to deal with the full load. With a surge of thankfulness almost light-headed, he got up and went over to the side table. On it lay a chart and a pair of dividers, ready for a job which, impelled by yet another of those queer fancies, he had sworn not to tackle until this moment arrived. The course for home. . . . He took out his pencil and prepared to calculate.

The only mark on the chart was Pilot's neat cross (too damned appropriate) marking their estimated position when the torpedo struck them, with the time and date—1630/31/12. From this he started to measure off.

Distance to the nearest of the Faeroes—210 miles, and nothing much when you got there. Distance to the nearest point of Britain—the Butt of Lewis, 270 miles. And just round the corner, another 30 miles or so—Stornoway. . . . That was the place to make for, he knew. It had no big repairing facilities, but it would be shelter enough, and they would be able to send tugs to bring them the rest of the way home. Stornoway—300 miles Say three knots. A hundred hours. Four days. Good enough.

Now for the course. The magnetic course, it must be: the master gyro-compass had been wrecked, and they would have to depend on the magnetic compasses, trusting that the explosion and the shifting of ballast had not put them out. South-east would do it. South-east for four days. Butt of Lewis was a good mark for them (he checked it on the chart): a flashing light, visible fourteen miles. That would bring them in all right. And what a landfall. . . .

When finally he laid down his pencil he was still in the same state of exaltation as had possessed him when he saw the lights come on. The desire to sleep had vanished: impelled to some sort of activity, he left the shelter of the

asdic hut and began to pace up and down outside. By God, once they got going there would
be no stopping them. . . . What did four days
matter?—they could keep going for four weeks
if it meant *Marlborough* making harbour at
the end. There was no depression now, no
morbid brooding about sacrifices or the cost
in men. It was *Marlborough* against the sea
and the enemy, and to-morrow would see her
cheating them both. He looked up at the sky,
clear and frosty: a night for action, for steering
small, for laughing and killing at the same
time. The first night of 1943. And to-morrow
they would sail into the new year like a prize-
fighter going in for the finish. Nothing was
going to stop them now.

Midday found them still drifting, still pow-
erless. A succession of minor breakdowns in-
volving in turn the fans and the steering-
engine held up everything during the morning:
at noon a defect in one of the oil pumps led
to more delay. The suspended activity, the
anti-climax after that first rush of feeling, was
a severe test of patience: it was with difficulty
that the Captain, walking the upper deck,
managed to exhibit a normal confidence. Part
of the morning was taken up with the burying

of two more men who had died during the night, but for the remainder he had little to occupy him; and as the afternoon advanced and the light declined, a dull stupor, matching his own indolence, seemed to envelop the ship. Stricken with the curse of immobility, she accepted the dusk as if it were all that her languor deserved.

Then, as swiftly as that first torpedo strike, the good news came. Chief, presenting himself in the wardroom with a cherful grin, announced that his repairs were complete: he used the classic formula "Ready to proceed, sir!" and he seemed to shed ten years in saying it. The Captain got up slowly, smiling in answer.

"Thank you, Chief. . . . A remarkable effort."

"We're all touching wood, sir." But he was almost boyish in his good humour.

"I want to start very gently. Twenty or thirty revs, not more. Will you put a reliable hand on the bulkhead?"

"I'll go myself, sir. The Chief E.R.A. can take charge in the engine-room."

"All right." The Captain raised his voice. "Pantry!"

The leading steward appeared.

"Ask Petty Officer Adams to come up to the bridge."

"Aye, aye, sir."

"I'll just ring 'Slow ahead' when I'm ready, Chief. We can do the rest by voice-pipe. If you hear anything at all from the bulkhead, stop engines straight away, of your own accord."

Within a minute or so he was on the bridge, the signalman by his side, Adams in the wheelhouse below. Leaning across the faintly lit compass he called down the voice-pipe:

"How's her head down there?"

"South, eighty west, sir."

The two compasses were in agreement. "Right. . . . Our course is south-east, Adams. Bring her round very slowly when we begin to move."

"Aye, aye, sir." Adams's voice, like the signalman's hard breathing at his elbow, reflected the tension that was binding them all.

The Captain took a deep breath. "Slow ahead starboard."

"Slow ahead starboard, sir."

The telegraph rang. There was a pause, then a slight tremor, then the beginning of a smooth pulsation. Very slowly *Marlborough* began to move. A thin ripple of bow-wave stood out in the luminous twilight: then another. In the compass bowl the floating disk stirred, edging away to the right. The ship started her turn, a slow, barely perceptible turn, 125 degrees to port in a wide half circle nearly a mile across.

Presently he called down the voice-pipe: "Steering all right?"

"Yes, sir. Five degrees of port wheel on."

The engine-room bell rang, and he bent to the voice-pipe, his throat constricted. "What is it?"

From the background of noise below an anonymous voice said: "Message from the engineer, sir. 'Nothing to report.' "

"Thank you."

A long pause, with nothing but smooth sliding movement. Then from Adams, suddenly: "Course—south-east, sir."

"Very good."

They were started. Forty-eight hours after the torpedoing: two days and two nights adrift. Course south-east.

The wind, now growing cold on the cheek, was like a caress.

That first night, those first fourteen hours of darkness on the bridge, had the intensity and the disquiet of personal dedication. It was as if he were taking hold of *Marlborough*—a sick, uncertain, but brave accomplice—and nursing her through the beginnings of a desperate convalescence. He rarely stirred from his chair, because he could see all he wanted from there —the sagging fo'c'sle, the still rigid bows—and he could hear and feel all the subtleties of her movement forward: but occasionally he stepped to the wing of the bridge and glanced aft, where their pale wake glittered and spread. Of all that his eyes could rest on, that was the most heartening. . . . Then back to his chair, and the stealthy advance of the bows, and the perpetual humming under-current that came from the engine-room voice-pipe, as comforting as the steady beat of an aircraft engine in mid-ocean. He was not in the least tired: sustained by love and hope, he felt ready to lend to *Marlborough* all his reserves of endurance.

At midnight the Chief came up to join him. His report was good: the engine had settled down, the bulkhead seemed unaffected by their forward movement. They discussed the idea of increasing speed, and decided against it: the log showed a steady three knots, sufficient for his plans.

"There's no point in taking bigger chances," said the Captain finally. "She's settled down so well that it would be stupid to fool about with the revs. I think we'll leave things as they are."

"Suits me, sir. It'll be a lot easier, seeing how shorthanded we are down there."

"You're working watch-and-watch, I suppose?"

"Got to, sir, with only two E.R.A.s. I'd stand a watch myself, but there's all the auxiliary machinery to look after." He yawned and stretched. "How about you, sir? Shall I give you a spell?"

"No, I'm all right, thanks, Chief. You turn in now, and get some sleep." The Captain smiled. "I always seem to be saying that to you. I hope you're doing it."

Chief smiled back. "Trust me, sir. Good night."

Presently, up the voice-pipe, came Adams's voice: "All right to hand over, sir?"

"Who's taking the wheel?"

"Leading Seaman Tapper, sir."

"All right, Adams. What does the steering feel like now?"

"A bit lumpy, sir. It takes a lot to bring her round if she starts swinging off. But it's nothing out of the way, really."

"I don't want anyone except you or Tapper to take the wheel until daylight."

"Aye, aye, sir."

It meant a long trick at the wheel for both these two; but inexpert steering might put too great a strain on the hull, and he wanted its endurance to be fully demonstrated before running any risks.

A moment later he heard the confirmatory "Course south-east—starboard engine slow ahead—Leading Seaman Tapper on the wheel," as Adams was relieved. Then the bridge settled down to its overall watchful tranquility again.

Indeed, his only other visitor, save for Bridger with a two-hourly relay of cocoa, was the doctor, who came up to tell him that the midshipman was dead. It was news which he had been waiting for, news with no element of surprise in it; but coming at a time of tension and weariness, toward the dawn, when he was cold and stiff and his eyes felt rimmed with tiredness, it was profoundly depressing. The midshipman, as captain's secretary, had spent a great deal of time with him: he was a cheerful, still irresponsible young man who had the makings of a first-class sailor. Now, at daylight, they would be burying him—and that only after alternate periods of agony and stupor, which had robbed death of every dignity. This, the latest and the most touching of the sacrifices that had been demanded of them, destroyed for the moment all the night's achievement.

Dawn restored it: a grey sunless dawn, only a lightening of the dull arch above them: but the new and blessed day for all that. As the gloom round them retreated and he was able to see, first the full outline of *Marlborough's* hull, then the shades of colour in the water, and then the horizon all round them, the triumph of the moment grew and warmed within him, dissolving all other feeling. By God, he thought, we can keep going for ever like this. . . . They were forty miles to the good already: there were only 260 more—three more nights, three more heartening dawns such as this: and *Marlborough,* creeping ahead over the smooth paling sea, was as strong as ever. If they could hold on to that (he touched the wood of his chair) then they were home.

At eight o'clock, the change of the watch, he called Leading Seaman Tapper to the bridge, and told him to turn over the wheel to the regular quartermaster and to take over as officer of the watch. It was irregular (he smiled as he realized how irregular), but he had to get some rest and there was no one else available to take his place: Chief was owed many hours of sleep, the doctor had been up all night with the midshipman, Adams had been on the wheel since four o'clock. It simply could not be helped.

He lay down at the back of the bridge, drew the hood of his duffle coat over his face, and closed his eyes against the frosty light. It was such bliss to relax at last, to sink away from care, that he found himself grinning foolishly. Fourteen hours on the bridge: and God knows how many the night before. . . . He would have to watch that. Might get the doc. to fix him up. Leading Seaman Tapper—*Acting*

Leading Seaman Tapper. . . . No, it couldn't be helped. In any case there was nothing to guard, nothing to watch for, nothing for them to fight with. Now, they had simply to endure.

Chapter Four

IT WAS at midday that the wind began to freshen, from the south.

The noise, slight as it was, woke the Captain. It began as no more than an occasional wave-slap against the bows, and a gentle lifting to the increased swell; but into his deep drugged sleep it stabbed like a sliver of ice. He lay still for a moment, getting the feel of the ship again, guessing at what· had happened: by the way *Marlborough* was moving, the wind was slightly off the bow, and already blowing crisply. Then he stood up, shook off his blankets, and walked to the front of the bridge.

It was as he had thought: a fresh breeze, curling the wave-top, was now meeting them, about twenty degrees off the starboard bow. Of the two, that was the better side, as it kept the torpedoed area under shelter: but the angle was still bad, it could still impart to their progress a twisting movement which might become a severe strain. While he was considering it, Adams came up to relieve Tapper, and they all three stood in silence for a moment, watching the waves as they slapped and broke against *Marlborough's* lowered bows.

"You'd better go back on the wheel, Adams," said the Captain presently. "If this gets any worse we'll have to turn directly into it, and slow down."

It did get worse, in the next hour he spent in his chair, and when the first wave, breaking right over the bows, splashed the fo'c'sle itself, he rang the bell to the engine-room. Chief himself answered.

"I'll have to take the revs off, Chief, I'm afraid," he said. "It's getting too lively altogether. What are they now?"

"Thirty-five, sir."

"Make that twenty. Have you got a hand on the bulkhead?"

"No, sir. I'll put one on."

"Right." He turned to the wheelhouse voice-pipe. "Steer south, twenty-five east, Adams. And tell me if she's losing steerage way. I want to keep the wind dead ahead."

"Aye, aye, sir."

The alteration, and the decrease in speed, served them well for an hour: then it suddenly seemed to lose its effect, and their movements became thoroughly strained and awkward. He decreased speed again, to fifteen revolutions—bare steerage-way—but still the awkwardness and the distress persisted: it became a steady thumping as each wave hit them, a recurrent lift-and-crunch which might have been specially designed to threaten their weakest point. It was now blowing steadily and strongly from the south: he listened to the wind rising with a murderous attention. At about half-past three it backed suddenly to the south-east, and he followed it: it meant they were heading for home again—the sole good point in a situation rapidly deteriorating. He looked at the seas running swiftly past them, and felt the ones breaking at the bows, and he knew that all their advantage was ebbing away from them. This was how it had been when he had been ready to abandon ship, three nights ago; it was this that was going to destroy them.

Quick steps rang on the bridge ladder, and he turned. It was the Chief: in the failing light his face looked grey and defeated.

"That bulkhead can't take this, sir," he began immediately. "I've been in to have a look, and it's started working again—there's the same leak down that seam. We'll have to stop."

The Captain shook his head. "That's no good, Chief. If we stop in this sea, we'll just bang ourselves to bits." A big wave hit them as he spoke, breaking down on the bows, driving them under. *Marlborough* came up from it very slowly indeed. "We've got to keep head to wind, at all costs."

"Can we go any slower, sir?"

"No. She'll barely steer as it is."

Another wave took them fair and square on the fo'c'sle, sweeping along the upper deck as *Marlborough* sagged into the trough. The wind tugged at them. It was as if the death-bed scene were starting all over again.

The Chief looked swiftly at the Captain. "Could we go astern into it?"

"Probably pull the bows off, Chief."

"Better than this, sir. This is just murder."

"Yes. . . . All right. . . . She may not come

round." He leant over to the voice-pipe. "Stop starboard."

"Stop starboard, sir." The telegraph clanged.

"Adams, I'm going astern, and up into the wind stern first. Put the wheel over hard a-starboard."

"Hard a-starboard, sir."

"Slow astern starboard."

The bell clanged again. "Starboard engine slow astern, wheel hard a-starboard, sir."

"Very good."

They waited. Those few minutes before *Marlborough* gathered stern way were horrible. She seemed to be standing in the jaws of the wind and sea, mutely undergoing a wild torture. She came down upon one wave with so solid a crash that it seemed impossible that the whole bows should not be wrenched off: a second, with a cruelty and malice almost deliberate, hit them a treacherous slewing blow on the port side. Slowly *Marlborough* backed away, shaking and staggering as if from a mortal thrust. The compass faltered, and started very slowly to turn: then as the wind caught the bows she began to swing sharply. He called out: "Watch it, Adams! Meet her! Bring her head on to north-west," and his hands as he gripped the pedestal were as white as the compass card. The last few moments, before *Marlborough* was safely balanced with her stern into the teeth of the wind, were like the sweating end of a nightmare.

Behind him the Chief sighed deeply. "Thank God for that. What revs do you want, sir?"

"We'll try twenty."

It was by now almost dark. *Marlborough* settled down to her awkward progress: both Adams and then Tapper wrestled steadily to keep her stern to the wind, while the waves mounted and steepened and broke solidly upon the quarterdeck. That whole night, which the Captain spent on the bridge, had a desperate quality of unrelieved distress. All the time the wind blew with great force from the south-east, all the time the seas ran against them as if powered by a living hate, and the vicious spray lashed the funnel and the bridge structure. At first light it began to snow: the driving clouds settled and lay thick all over them, crusting the upper deck in total icy whiteness. *Marlborough* might have been sailing backwards off a Christmas cake . . . but still, with unending, hopeless persistence, she butted her way southwards.

Five days later—one hundred and twenty-one hours—she was still doing it. The snow was gone, and the gale had eased to a stiff southerly breeze; but the sea was still running too high for them to risk turning their bows into it, and so they maintained, stern first, their ludicrous progress. The whole after-part of the ship had been drenched with water ever since they turned; the wardroom had been made uninhabitable by a leaking sky-light, the alley way in which the men slept was six inches awash with a frothy residue of spray. It was hardly to be wondered at, thought the Captain as he slopped through it on his way back to the bridge: poor old *Marlborough* hadn't been designed for this sort of thing.

He was very tired. He had hardly had two consecutive hours of sleep in the last five days: the strain had settled in his face like a tight and ugly mask. The doctor had done his best to relieve him, by taking an occasional spell on the bridge when the remaining four serious patients could be left; but even this seemed of no avail—his weariness, and the hours of concentration on *Marlborough's* foolish movements, pursued him like a hypnosis, twitching his eyelids when he sought sleep, making his scalp prickle and the brain inside flutter. Hope of rest was destroyed by a twanging tension such as sometimes made him want to scream aloud. When he sat down in his chair on that fifth night of sternway—the ninth since they were torpedoed—and hunched his stiff shoulders against the cold, he was conscious of nothing save an appalling lassitude. Even to stare and search ahead, in quest of those shore-lights that never showed themselves, was effort enough to make him feel sick in doing it.

He had no idea where they were. They had seen nothing—no lights at night, no aircraft, not a single smudge of smoke anywhere on the horizon. The sextant had been smashed by the shellfire, and there was no sun anyway to take sights by. Even at two knots, even at one-and-a-half, they should have raised Butt of Lewis light by now, if their course were correct. That was the hellish, the insane part of it. Probably it wasn't correct: probably the torpedoing and the weight-shifting had put everything out, and the magnetic compasses were completely haywire. Probably they were heading straight out into the Atlantic instead of pointing for home. And Christ! he thought, this bloody cock-eyed way of steaming . . . you couldn't tell where the ship was going to. They might be anywhere. They might be going round in circles, digging their own grave.

Bridger, the admirable unassailable Bridger, appeared at his elbow. The cup of cocoa which seemed to be part of his right arm was once more tendered. While he drank it, Bridger stood in silence, looking out at the sea. Then he said:

"Easing off a bit, sir."

"Just a little, yes."

There was another pause: then Bridger added: "It's a lot drier aft, sir."

"Good." It was impossible not to respond to this effort at raising his spirits, or to be unaffected by it; and he said suddenly: "What do the hands think about all this?" It was the sort of question he had never before asked any rating except the Coxswain.

Bridger considered. It was entirely novel to him, too; what the lower deck thought of things, and what they said about them to their officers, were two differing aspects of truth. At length:

"They're a bit sick of the corned beef, sir."

The Captain laughed, for the first time for many days. "Is that all?"

"Just about, sir. But we're having a sweepstake on when we get in."

For some reason the Captain felt like crying at that one. He said, after a moment:

"Has your number come up yet?"

"No, sir. Six more days to run."

There was much more that the Captain wanted to ask: did they really think *Marlborough* would get in: were they still confident in his judgment, after all these days and nights of blundering along: did they trust him absolutely?—questions he would never ever have thought of, save in a lightheaded hunger for reassurance. But suddenly Bridger said:

"They hope you're getting enough sleep, sir!"

Then he sucked in his breath, as though discovered in some appalling breach of discipline, took the cup from the top of the compass, and quickly left the bridge. Alone once more, the Captain smiled tautly at the most moving thing that had ever been said to him, and settled back in his chair to take up the watch again. He *wasn't* getting enough sleep, but the fact that the ship's company realized this, and wished him well over it, was as sustaining and comforting as a strong arm round his shoulders.

On the morning of the tenth day since they were torpedoed, he had a conference with the Chief on the bridge. They had seen little of each other during the preceding time: five days of having the reversing gear in continuous action had proved an unaccustomed strain, and the Chief had been kept busy below, nursing the one remaining engine through its ordeal. Now, at nine o'clock, he had come up with some fresh news.

"Have you noticed the fo'c'sle, sir?"

"No, Chief, I hadn't." After yet another night on the bridge he felt no more and no less tired than usual: he semed to be living in some nether hell of weariness which nothing could deepen. What's happened to it?"

"The bows have started to bend upwards again." He pointed. "You can just about see it from here, sir. There's a kink in the deck, like folding a bit of paper."

"You mean the whole thing's being pulled off."

"Something like that, sir. It's a slow process,

but if it gets any worse we'll lose the buoyancy of the forepeak, and that may bring the screws out of the water again.

"What's the answer, technically?"

"Either slow down to nothing, or turn round and push them on again."

The Captain gestured irritably. "My God, it's like fooling around with a bundle of scrap-iron! 'Push the bows on again'—it sounds like some blasted lid off a tin!"

"Yes, sir." While Chief waited for the foolish spasm to spend itself, he wondered idly what the Captain *really* thought *Marlborough* should be like, after what she had gone through. "Bundle of scrapiron" wasn't far wide of the mark: she could float, she could lollop backwards, and that was about all. "Well, that's the choice, sir," he said presently. "I don't think we can carry on like this much longer."

The Captain got hold of himself again: at this late hour, he wasn't going to start dramatizing the situation. It was all this damned tiredness. . . . "We could just about turn round now," he said slowly, looking at the sea with its long rolling swell and occasional breaking wave-tops. "It was a lot worse than this before we turned last time."

"And how far have we got to go, Sir?"

"I don't know, Chief." He did not make the mistake of admitting his ignorance in a totally normal voice, but he managed to imply that there was nothing to be gained either by a full discussion of it, or by surrendering to its hopeless implication. "If we were on our proper course we should have raised Butt of Lewis a long time ago. Probably the compasses are faulty. I'm just going to keep on like this till we hit something."

Stopping, and turning the bows into the wind again, was an even slower process than it had been five days earlier: at times it seemed that *Marlborough*, lying lumpishly off the wind and butting those fragile bows against the run of the waves, *would not* come up to her course. The Captain dared not increase speed, in order to give the rudder more leverage; and so for a full half-hour they tumbled athwart the wave-troughs, gaining a point on the compass-card, sagging back again, wavering on and off the wind like a creaking weathercock that no one trusts any longer. Down in the wheelhouse, Leading Seaman Tapper leant against the wheel which he had put hard a-starboard, and waited, his eyes on the compass-card. If she wouldn't, she wouldn't: no good worrying, no good fiddling about. . . . All over the ship, during the past few days, that sort of thing had been growing: things either went right, or they didn't, and that was all there was to it. Between a deep weariness and a deeper fatalism, the whole crew accepted the situation, and were carried sluggishly along with it.

At the end of half an hour a lull allowed *Marlborough* to come round on her course. She settled down again slowly, as if she did not really believe in it, but knew she had no choice. South-east, it was, and one and a half knots. It *must* bring them home. It had to.

It did not bring them home: it did not seem to bring them anywhere. They steamed all that day, and all the next, and all the next, and all the next: four more days and nights, to add to the fantastic total of that south-easterly passage. But *was* it a south-easterly passage?—for if so, they should by now have been right through Scotland, and out the other side: eleven days steaming, it added up to, and thirteen days since they had been torpedoed. It just didn't make sense.

The weather did not help. It did not deteriorate, it did not improve: the stiff breeze held all the time, the sloppy uneven sea came running at them for hour after hour and day after day. The ship took it all with a tough determination which could not disguise a steady progressive breaking down. The bulkhead wavered and creaked, the water ran down the splitting seam, slopped about on the deck, increased in weight till it began to drag the bows down to a fatal level. The noise mounted gradually to an appalling racket: clanging, groaning, knocking, protesting—the whole hull in pain, ill-treated as an old galled horse sweating against the collar, fit only for the knacker's yard but hardly strong enough to drag itself there. Gallant, ramshackle, on her last legs, *Marlborough* bumped and rolled southwards, at a pace which was itself a wretched trial of patience.

Above all, there was now a smell—a sweetish, sickish smell seeping up the ventilators from the fo'c'sle. It penetrated to every part of the ship, it hung in the wind, it followed them till there seemed to be nothing around them in the sea or the sky but the gross stink of the dead, those seventy-odd corpses which they carried with them as their obscene ballast. It could not be escaped anywhere in the ship. Every man on board lived with it, tried to shut it out with sleep, woke with it sweet and beastly in his nostrils. It became the unmentionable horror that attended them wherever they went.

They all hated it, but there was so much more to hate. The tiredness of overstrained men working four hours on and four hours off, for day after day and night after night, lay all over the ship, a tangible weight of weariness that affected every yard of their progress. The ship's company, whether watching on the upper deck or tending the boilers and the engine room, moved in a tired dream barely distinguishable from sleep. A grotesque fatigue assailed them all: they stayed on watch till their eyes ran raw and their bodies seemed ready to crumple: they ate like men who could scarcly move their jaws against some dry and tasteless substance: they fell asleep where they dropped, wedged against ventilators, curled up like bundles of rags in odd corners of the deck. All of them were filthy, bearded, grimed with spray and smoke: there was no water to wash with, no change of clothes, nothing to hearten them but tea and hard biscuit and corned beef, for every meal of every day of the voyage. All over the ship one met them, or stumbled over them: wild-eyed, dirty, slightly mad. And all round them, and above and below, hung that smell of death, a thick enveloping curtain, the price of sea-power translated into a squalid and disgusting currency.

And the Captain . . . he summed up, in his person, all that tiredness, all that stress and dirt, all that wild fatigue. He had had the least sleep of any one on board, throughout the thirteen days: at the end of it he still held the whole thing in his grip, but it was a grip that had another quality besides strength—it had something cracked and desperate about it. His was the worry, his the responsibility, his the appalling doubt as to whether they were really going anywhere at all: he held on because there was no choice, because they could not give up, above all because this was *Marlborough,* his own ship, and he would not surrender her to God or man or the sea. Like a lover, light-headed and despairing, he hoped and strove and would not be foresworn.

The bridge was now his prison. . . . Wedged in his chair, chin on hand, a small thing was beginning to obsess him. On one of the instruments in front of him there was a splash of dried blood, overlooked when they cleaned up after the shell-burst. It had an odd shape, like a boot, like Italy: but the silly thing was that when he looked to one side that shape seemed to change, spinning round and round like a windmill, expanding and contracting as if the blood still lived and still moved to a pulse. He tried to catch it moving, but when he stared at it directly it became Italy again, a dirty brownish smear that no one wanted. He roared out suddenly: "Signalman!" and then: "For Christ's sake clean that off—its filthy!" and when the man, staring, set to work on the job, he watched him as if his sanity depended on it. Then he looked ahead again, scanning the horizon, the damned crystal-clear horizon. No change there: no shadow, no smudge of smoke, nothing. Where were they going to? Was there anything ahead but deep water? Was he leading *Marlborough*, and the wretched remnant of her ship's company, on a fantastic chase into the blue? And God Almighty! That smell from forrard. . . . It was like a curse, clamped down hard on their necks. Perhaps they were all going to perish of it in the end: perhaps the whole ship and her dead and dying crew, welded together in a solid mass of corruption, would one night dip soundlessly beneath the sea and touch bottom a thousand fathoms below.

At 4 a.m. on the morning of January 14 Petty Officer Adams came up on the bridge, to see the Captain before taking over the wheel. He had a pair of binoculars slung beneath the hood of his duffle coat, and from force of habit he raised them and swept slowly round the horizon, a barely distinguishable line of shadow on that black moonless night. He did this twice: then, on the verge of lowering his glasses, he checked suddenly and stared for a long minute ahead, blinking at the rawness, the watery eyestrain, which even this slight effort induced. Then he said, in a compressed, almost croaking voice:

"There's a light dead ahead, sir."

The words fell into the silence on the bridge like a rock in a pool. They all whipped up their glasses and stared in turn—the Captain, the signalman, Bridger, with his cocoa cup forgotten: all of them intent, tremendously alert, checking their breathing as if afraid of losing an instant's concentration. Then Adams said again:

"There it is, sir—only the loom of it, but you can see it sweeping across."

And the Captain, answering him, said very softly: "Yes."

It *was* a light—the faintest lifting of the gloom in the sky, like a spectral fan opening and closing, like a whisper—but it *was* a light. For a moment, the Captain was childishly annoyed that he had not seen it first: and then a terrific and overpowering relief seemed to rise in his throat, choking him, pricking his eyes, flooding all over his body in a shaking spasm. The soreness which he had felt round his heart all through the last few days rose to an agonizing twinge and then fell away, leaving him weak, almost gasping. He found the light again, and then dropped his binoculars and leant against his chair. The wish to cry, at the end of the fourteen days' tension, was almost insupportable.

Round him the others reacted in their own way, contributing to a moment of release so extraordinary that no extravagance of move-

ment or word could have been out of place.
The cup which Bridger had placed on a ledge
fell and shattered. The signalman was whist-
ling an imitation of a bosun's pipe, a trium-
phant skirl of sound. Adams, unknowing, mut-
tered: "Jesus Christ, Jesus Christ, Jesus
Christ," over and over again, in a voice from
which everything save a sober humility had
disappeared. They were men in a moment
of triumph and of weakness, as vulnerable as
young chidren, as unstable, as near to ecstasy
or to weeping in the same single breath. They
were men in entrancement.

It *was* a light—and soon there were others:
three altogether, winking and beckoning them
towards the vast promise of the horizon. The
Captain took a grip of himself, the tightest
grip yet, and went into the charthouse to work
them out; while all over the ship men, awak-
ened by some extraordinary urgency which
ran everywhere like a licking flame, leant over
the rails, and stared and whispered and
laughed at what they saw. Lights ahead—land—
home—they'd made it after all. Some of them
stared up at the bridge, seeing nothing but
feeling that they were looking at the heart of
the ship, the thing that had brought them

home, the man who more than anyone had worked the miracle. And then they would go back to the lights again, and count the flashes, and start singing or cursing in ragged chorus. There was no one anywhere in the ship who did not share in this moment: the hands on the upper deck shouted the news down to the engine-room, the signalman on the bridge gave a breathless running commentary to the wheelhouse. The release from ordeal moved them all to the same wild exaltation.

Only the Captain, faced by the array of charts on the table, no longer shared the full measure of their relief. For he was now concentrating on something else, something he could not make out at all. They were lights all right—but what lights? The one that Adams had first seen was not Butt of Lewis: the other two did not seem to fit any part of the chart, either Lewis or the mainland round Cape Wrath, or the scattered islands centred on Scapa Flow and the Orkneys. He checked them again, he laid off the bearings on a piece of tracing-paper and then moved it here and there on the chart, hesitatingly, like a child with its first jigsaw puzzle. He even moved it up to Iceland, but the answer would not come—and it was an answer they *must* have before very long: they were running into something, closing an unknown coastline which might have any number of hazards—outlying rocks, dangerous overfalls, minefields barring any approach except by a single swept channel. Sucking his pencil, frowning at the harsh lamplight, he strove to find the answer: even at this last moment, delay might rob them of their triumph. But the answer would not come.

Presently he opened the charthouse door and came out again, ready to take fresh bearings and to make doubly certain of what the lights showed. Both the doctor and the Chief were now on the bridge, talking in low voices through which ran a strong note of satisfaction and assurance. The Chief turned as he heard the step, and then jerked his head at the lights.

"Finest sight I've seen in my life, sir."

The Captain smiled. "Same here, Chief."

"Is that Butt of Lewis, sir?" asked the doctor.

"No." He raised his glasses, checked the number of the flashes, and bent to the compass to take a fresh bearing. "No, Doc, I haven't worked out what it is yet."

"It's something solid, anyway."

"Enough for me," said the Chief. "All I

121

want is the good old putty, anywhere between Cape Wrath and the Longships."

To himself the Captain thought: I wish I could guarantee that.

"Another light, sir!" exclaimed the signalman suddenly. "Port bow—about four-oh."

The Captain raised his glasses once more.

"There it is, sir," said the signalman again, before the Captain had found it. "It's a red one this time."

"Red?"

"Yes, sir. I got it clearly then."

Red . . . that rang a bell, by God! There was a red light at the end of Rathlin Island, of the north coast of Ireland: it was the only one he could remember, in fact. But Rathlin Island. He walked quickly into the charthouse, and moved the tracing paper southwards. The jigsaw suddenly resolved itself. It *was* Rathlin: the light they had first seen was Inistrahull, the others were Inishowen and something else he could not check—probably an aircraft beacon. Rathlin Island—that meant that they had come all down the coast of Scotland, over two hundred miles farther than he had thought: it meant that they must have been steering at least fifteen degrees off their proper course.

Those bloody compasses! But what did it matter now? Rathlin Island. They could put in at Londonderry and get patched up, and then go home. Nothern Ireland instead of Butt of Lewis—that would look good in the Report. But what the hell *did* it matter? They had made their landfall.

He walked back to his chair, sat down, and said, in as level a voice as he had ever used:

"That's the north coast of Ireland. "We'll be going to Derry."

It was a peerless morning: the clean grey sky, flecked with pearly grey clouds, turned suddenly to gold as the sun climbed over the eastern horizon. There was now land ahead: a dark bluish coastline, with noble hills beyond. The Captain's stiff stubbly face warmed slowly to the sunshine: the ache across his shoulders and round his heart semed to melt away, taking with it his desperate fatigue. Not much longer—and then sleep, and sleep, and sleep. . . . Bridger handed him the morning cup of cocoa, his face one enormous grin. But all he said was: "Cocoa, sir."

"Thanks. . . . We made it, Bridger."

"Yes, sir."

"Who won that sweepstake?"

"The Buffer, sir—I mean, Petty Officer Adams."

The Captain laughed aloud. "Bad luck!" For the ship's company that must be the one flaw in an otherwise perfect morning. There were a lot of the hands on the upper deck now, smiling and pointing. He felt bound to them as closely as one man can be to another. Later, he wanted to find some words that would give them an idea of that. And something about *Marlborough*, too, the ship he loved, the ship they had all striven for.

"Trawlers ahead, sir," said the signalman, breaking in on his thoughts. "Three of them. I think they're sweeping."

Back to civilization: to lights, harbours, dawn mine-sweepers, patrolling aircraft, a guarded fairway.

"Call them up, signalman."

But one of the trawlers was already flashing to them. The signalman acknowledged the message, and said: "From the trawler, sir: 'Can I help you?' "

"Make: 'Thank you. Are you going into Londonderry?' "

A pause, while the lamps flickered. Then: "Reply 'Yes,' sir!"

"Right. Make: 'Will you pass a message to the Port War Signal Station for me, please?' "

Another pause. "Reply, 'Certainly,' sir."

The Captain drew a long breath, conscious deep within him of an enormous satisfaction. "Write this down, and then send it to them. 'To Flag Officer in Charge, Londonderry, v. *Marlborough*. H.M.S. *Marlborough* will enter harbour at 1300 to-day. Ship is severly damaged above and below waterline. Request pilot, tugs, dockyard assistance, and burial arrangements for one officer and seventy-four ratings.' Got that?"

"Yes, sir."

"Right. Send it off. . . . Bridger!"

"Sir?"

"Ask the surgeon-lieutenant to relieve me for an hour. I'm going to shave. And wash. And change. And then eat."

FROM THE BEST-SELLING AUTHOR OF
"THE CRUEL SEA"

NICHOLAS MONSARRAT

A superb account of the hunting of subs
in the darkest days of the war

THREE CORVETTES

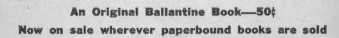